THE FATMAN

NOT ALL GIFTS ARE MEANT TO BE OPENED. NOT ALL BELIEFS ARE MEANT TO SURVIVE. AND IN THE ETERNAL COLD, EVEN SANTA CLAUS HAS TEETH. HO...HO...HO...

Patti Petrone Miller

COPYRIGHT © NOVEMBER 2024 BY PATTI PETRONE MILLER
No part of this publication may be reproduced, stored in a retrieval system, or transmitted, in any form or by any means, without the prior permission in writing of the publisher, nor be otherwise circulated in any form of binding or cover other than that in which it is published and without a similar condition including this condition being imposed on the subsequent purchaser.

FBI Anti-Piracy Warning: The unauthorized reproduction or distribution of a copyrighted work is illegal.

Criminal copyright infringement, including infringement without monetary gain, is investigated by the FBI and is punishable by up to five years in federal prison and a fine of $250,000.

(THE FATMAN) First Edition

Cover art by GRADY EARLS

Published by AP Miller Productions All rights reserved.

YOUR SUPPORT OF THE AUTHOR'S RIGHTS IS APPRECIATED.

THE FATMAN

FOR ALL MY PUPPIES LOVED SPOILED AND NEVER FORGOTTEN

THE FATMAN

BY PATTI PETRONE MILLER

Authors Book List

Accidental Vows
A Krampus Christmas
Sin Takes A Holiday
Barking Up The Wrong Bakery, Thankgiving
Barking Up The Wrong Bakery, Christmas
Best Served Dead
Bewitching Charms
Christmas at Hollybrook Inn
Christmas on Peppermit Lane
Krampus
Hex and the City
Love in Stitches
Pies and Perps
Spectres and Souffles
Mamma Mia It's Murder
Once Upon A Christmas
The Fatman
The Frosted Felony
The Purr-fect Suspect
The Boogeyman
The Gingerdead Men
Vikings Enchantress
Welcome to Scarecrow Hollow
The Pendleton Witches
The Cabinet of Curiosities
Christmas In Pine Haven
Love in the Stacks
Once Upon A Christmas

Patti Petrone Miller

THE FATMAN

CHAPTER 1
THE AUGUR'S WARNING

Blood on fresh snow formed perfect circles, each drop a crimson prophecy in the pristine white. Jinx Tinsel's brass-and-silver fingers whirred as she traced the pattern, her clockwork augmentations detecting vibrations deep beneath the frozen ground. The mechanical runes etched into her left hand glowed faintly, reading signatures of magic that no ordinary elf could sense.

Something was wrong at Polaris Keep.

The ancient fortress of the Winter King rose before her, its crystalline spires refracting the ethereal dance of the aurora borealis. But tonight, the usual emerald and sapphire lights writhed with threads of scarlet—a color never before seen in the Northern Lights. Her clockwork heart ticked faster, its intricate gears responding to the surge of adrenaline.

The warning bells should have been ringing. The magical wards should have flared. Yet the night remained silent save for the bitter wind that carried the scent of ancient magic gone sour.

Jinx pressed her mechanical palm flat against the snow, sending out a pulse of clockwork magic. The brass gears embedded in her forearm spun rapidly, translating the magical frequencies into comprehensible data. What she read in those vibrations made her artificial joints lock with dread.

The Winter's Crown was failing.

THE FATMAN

She sprinted toward the fortress gates, her enhanced legs carrying her across the snow in long, graceful bounds. The guards—typically as vigilant as statues—were nowhere to be seen. The massive doors of enchanted ice stood partially open, another anomaly that sent warnings cascading through her mechanical augmentations.

The entrance hall stretched before her, its vaulted ceiling lost in shadows that seemed to writhe with unnatural movement. Jinx's left hand hummed as it detected traces of foreign magic, like oil floating on clear water. The elegant ice sculptures that lined the corridor—normally depicting scenes of winter wonder—had begun to twist into grotesque shapes.

"Your Majesties!" Her voice echoed through the empty halls. "My King! My Queen!"

The only response was a distant sound of breaking glass.

Jinx raced toward the throne room, her brass joints gleaming in the strange light. The temperature dropped with each step, far below even the usual arctic cold of Polaris Keep. This wasn't the natural chill of winter—this was the kind of cold that belonged to the void between realms.

The doors to the throne room had been frozen shut, not by the usual orderly magic of the Winter King, but by chaotic ice that sprawled like black veins across the surface. Jinx's mechanical hand transformed, gears shifting until her fingers became delicate tools. She pressed them to the ice, sending pulses of clockwork magic to probe for weaknesses.

A scream shattered the silence—Mrs. Claus's voice, filled with a fury that made the very foundations of the fortress tremble.

Jinx abandoned precision for power. She slammed her mechanized fist into the ice, channeling every ounce of magical energy her clockwork augmentations could generate. The door exploded inward in a shower of crystalline shards.

The scene before her defied centuries of natural law.

The Winter's Crown—source of Santa's power to traverse the realms—hovered above his empty throne. But instead of its usual platinum and diamond splendor, the crown was webbed with veins of crimson energy. As Jinx watched in horror, a crack appeared in one of its ancient gems, releasing a sound like a thousand breaking bells.

Mrs. Claus stood in the center of the room, her white hair writhing with magical power, her hands weaving spells of containment around the crown. But the magic was failing, unraveling like rot-weakened thread.

"Jinx!" The Winter Queen's voice carried the weight of command. "The arcanometric readings—quickly!"

Jinx's mechanical arms reconfigured, brass panels sliding aside to reveal delicate instruments. She began to take measurements of the crown's deteriorating magic, but the readings made no sense. The numbers shifted chaotically, suggesting patterns that should have been impossible.

"My Queen, these readings..." Jinx's clockwork heart skipped a gear. "This isn't natural decay. The crown's being corrupted from within, but the signature... it's not possible."

"What signature?" Mrs. Claus demanded, sweat freezing on her brow as she fought to contain the crown's unstable energy.

Before Jinx could respond, a sound deeper than sound itself reverberated through the chamber. The crown's largest gem cracked, and from within that fissure came a laugh that had haunted winter legends for millennia.

The temperature plummeted. Ice crept across the walls, not the elegant fractal patterns of the Winter King's magic, but twisted, thorny growths that seemed to drink in light itself. The crimson aurora outside blazed brighter, casting the throne room in the color of fresh blood.

"Where is he?" Jinx demanded, her voice barely steady. "Where is Santa?"

Mrs. Claus's face was a mask of concentrated fury, but Jinx caught the flicker of fear in her expression. "The Void Gate," she said through gritted teeth. "He's trying to reinforce the seals, but—"

Another crack appeared in the Winter's Crown, and with it came a wave of power that knocked them both backward. Jinx's mechanical legs whirred as they compensated, keeping her upright. Her sensors screamed with readings that threatened to overwhelm her augmentations.

From within the crown's fractured gems, a voice spoke—ancient, cruel, and filled with triumph.

"The seal is broken, dear sister," it said, addressing Mrs. Claus. "Your king's reign ends tonight."

The crown shattered.

THE FATMAN

A blast of void-cold magic exploded outward as reality itself seemed to tear. Jinx threw up a clockwork shield, protecting herself and Mrs. Claus from the worst of it. When the magical storm cleared, her sensors detected a presence that should have been impossible.

There, within the fragments of the Winter's Crown, a shadowy form began to take shape. Horns curved up toward the vaulted ceiling. Claws of ancient darkness reached toward the mortal realm.

Krampus was returning.

And Santa was nowhere to be found.

The shadowy form solidified, darkness coalescing into ancient flesh. Krampus's presence filled the throne room like smoke, his massive horns scraping against the vaulted ceiling. The twisted staff he gripped writhed with the same corruption that had infected the Winter's Crown, its surface crawling with symbols that made Jinx's mechanical sensors malfunction.

"How long I've waited, sister," Krampus said, his voice resonating at frequencies that made the crystalline walls vibrate. "How long I've watched from the void while you and your king played at ruling winter." He stepped forward, each footfall leaving frost-blackened marks on the floor. "Did you really think your binding spell would hold forever?"

Mrs. Claus raised her hands, frost gathering around her fingers. "Back to your prison, brother. You have no place in this realm."

Jinx's clockwork heart measured each second with painful precision as she analyzed the situation. Her mechanical augmentations detected power readings that threatened to overwhelm her sensors. Krampus radiated magic that felt wrong—discordant frequencies that made her brass joints ache and her artificial synapses misfire.

The Winter Queen's spell lashed out, a cascade of pristine ice meant to entrap and banish. But Krampus caught the magic in one clawed hand, crushing it. The broken fragments fell like black snow.

"Your magic is bound to his crown, sister. And now..." He gestured to the shattered remains of the Winter's Crown. "Well, even queens must bow to changing times."

Jinx's mind raced through calculations, her clockwork enhancements processing possible strategies. The crown pieces still held residual magic—she could sense it. If she could just reach them, perhaps her mechanical expertise could—

Movement caught her attention. In the shadows behind Krampus, a figure darted between the pillars. Jinx caught a glimpse of crimson robes, white beard stained with frost. Santa had returned from the Void Gate. But something was wrong. He moved like a wounded man, trailing magic that sparked and fizzled erratically.

Mrs. Claus must have seen him too. She straightened, drawing herself to her full height. "You were always poor at arithmetic, brother. Let me offer you a lesson in counting." Her voice carried the weight of millennia. "How many rulers does the Winter Court require?"

Krampus laughed, the sound like breaking icicles. "One. After tonight, only one."

"Wrong." Mrs. Claus smiled, and it was not a kind expression. "The answer is two. A king and queen, working in harmony. Take one away..." Her hands moved in complex patterns. "And the other's power doubles."

She brought her hands together with a thunderous crack. The temperature plummeted so rapidly that even Jinx's cold-resistant augmentations screamed warnings. Ice erupted from every surface—walls, floor, ceiling—but this was not the ordered magic of before. This was ancient winter unleashed, primal and hungry.

Krampus staggered back, genuine surprise crossing his shadowed features. "What have you done?"

"A queen's final resort," Mrs. Claus said through gritted teeth. "Jinx, the crown fragments! Now!"

Jinx launched herself forward, mechanical legs propelling her across the ice-slick floor. Her brass fingers transformed into delicate tools as she slid past Krampus, snatching up pieces of the shattered crown. Each fragment hummed with residual power, resonating with her clockwork magic in ways she'd never felt before.

Behind her, Krampus roared. The sound carried undertones that made her mechanical systems stutter and glitch. She heard Mrs. Claus cry out in pain.

Time slowed as Jinx's augmented senses processed the scene. Santa, moving with desperate speed despite his injuries. Mrs. Claus, her power flooding the chamber with killing cold. Krampus, reaching for his twisted staff with murderous intent. And between them all, scattered across the floor, the fragments of a crown that had maintained the balance of winter for countless centuries.

THE FATMAN

The pieces in Jinx's mechanical hand pulsed with possibility. Her clockwork magic detected patterns in the fragments—a hidden frequency that suggested they could be reformed. Not as they were, perhaps, but as something new. Something that might save them all, or doom them completely.

If she could just figure out the pattern in time.

A blast of void-cold magic swept through the chamber. Jinx's augmentations registered a catastrophic drop in temperature mere moments before her mechanical joints began to freeze.

The last thing she saw was Santa stepping from the shadows, his hands raised to cast a spell she'd never seen before—one that made her clockwork heart stop its measured ticking for the first time since her transformation.

Then darkness took the world, and the real winter began.

Chapter 2
Fractured Magic

Consciousness returned to Jinx in calculated increments. Her clockwork heart resumed its ticking—slower than normal, each metallic beat labored against the lingering cold. Diagnostic routines activated automatically, sending status reports through her augmented nervous system. Multiple systems compromised. Magical resonance detectors offline. Brass joints operating at thirty percent efficiency.

The throne room lay in ruins around her. Sheets of black ice covered the walls, crawling with corrupt sigils that made her mechanical sensors spark with interference. Where the Winter's Crown had shattered, the floor was scorched with patterns that suggested violent spellwork.

Mrs. Claus was gone. So was Krampus. And Santa...

Memory fragments reassembled themselves: Santa emerging from the shadows, his hands raised in that final, unknown spell. The magic he'd wielded hadn't felt like his usual power. It had resonated at frequencies that belonged to older, darker winters.

Jinx forced her joints to move, brass fingers scraping against the frozen floor as she pushed herself upright. The crown fragments she'd gathered were still clutched in her mechanical hand, their edges cutting into the metal of her palm. Each piece hummed with discordant energy, like instruments playing in clashing keys.

"Your Majesties?" Her voice echoed through the empty chamber. Static crackled in her artificial vocal cords, an aftereffect of the magical surge that had knocked her offline.

No response. But her sensors, though damaged, detected residual magic concentrated near the throne. She stumbled toward it, her enhanced legs struggling to compensate for the uneven, ice-slick floor.

The throne itself had transformed. What had once been an elegant seat of crystalline ice was now a twisted spire of obsidian frost. Carved into its surface were runes that predated the Winter Kingdom itself—symbols that spoke of magic from the first winter, when the boundaries between realms had been thinner.

Something glinted at the throne's base. Jinx knelt, her brass joints protesting the movement. Half-buried in the black ice was a small brass key, worked with intricate clockwork patterns that matched her own augmentations. But she had never seen this key before.

Her mechanical hand moved automatically to retrieve it. The moment her fingers touched the metal, information flooded her systems. Coordinates. Frequencies. Magical formulae that made her processors strain to comprehend. And beneath it all, a message encoded in mechano-magical algorithms that only she could read:

The crown was always meant to break. Find me in the Workshop of Winter's First Dawn.

The message bore Santa's magical signature, but it was fragmented, corrupted by interference from some other power source. More troubling was the timestamp encoded within it. According to the magical metadata, Santa had created this message three months ago.

He had known this was coming.

A grinding sound drew her attention to the throne room's far wall. The ice there was shifting, forming a doorway that hadn't existed before. Through it, Jinx glimpsed stone stairs descending into darkness. The steps were worn with age, suggesting they had existed long before Polaris Keep was built.

Her diagnostic systems finally completed their full damage assessment. Beyond the mechanical issues, something fundamental had changed within her. The clockwork magic that powered her augmentations felt different—wilder, less constrained by the natural laws she had always taken for granted. It was as if the shattering of the Winter's Crown had broken more than just itself.

A sound like distant bells echoed up from the stairwell. Not the pure, clear chime of Christmas magic, but something darker. Ancient. Hungry.

Jinx accessed her mental archives, searching historical records stored in her mechanical memory. The Workshop of Winter's First Dawn appeared in only one text: a fragment of pre-kingdom lore that spoke of the place where the first winter crafters had forged their magic. The location had been lost for millennia.

Until now.

She looked down at the crown fragments in her hand. Even damaged, they held immense power. Power that, according to everything she had been taught, should have killed her when the crown shattered. Yet here she stood, her clockwork heart still ticking.

Why had Santa left her this key? Why encode a message that could only be read by her specific combination of mechanical and magical abilities? And most troubling of all—if he had known this catastrophe was coming, why hadn't he prevented it?

Another sound echoed up the stairwell, closer this time. Something was ascending from those ancient depths. Her damaged sensors couldn't get a clear reading, but the magical resonance made her artificial synapses misfire with recognition.

The void-cold magic carried Krampus's signature.

Jinx ran quick calculations. Her systems were too damaged for direct confrontation. The crown fragments needed to be protected. And that key... The coordinates it contained led somewhere in the Winterspine Mountains, far from Polaris Keep.

A third sound rang out, closer still. No longer bells, but laughter. Ancient. Cruel. Triumphant.

Decision made, Jinx turned toward the throne room's secret exit—a passage known only to the keep's master artificer. As she moved, she caught her reflection in a sheet of black ice. Her mechanical components gleamed dully, frost crawling across their brass surfaces. But it was her organic eye that gave her pause.

Where once it had glowed with standard elfin magic, it now shone with the same crimson light that had infected the aurora. Something of that final spell—Santa's impossible magic—had changed her on a fundamental level.

THE FATMAN

The passage door sealed behind her just as heavy footsteps entered the throne room. Through the wall, she heard Krampus's voice, thick with malice: "Find the artificer. The crown fragments must not reach the Workshop."

Jinx's clockwork heart beat faster as she hurried through the hidden corridor. The passage would take her to the lower vaults, where the keep's most experimental devices were stored. She would need weapons for what was coming. Tools. Anything that might help her understand what Santa had known, and why he had chosen her for this mission.

The key grew colder in her mechanical hand, its encoded coordinates pulsing like a heartbeat. Somewhere in the Winterspine Mountains, the Workshop of Winter's First Dawn waited. And with it, perhaps, answers to questions she hadn't even known to ask.

Behind her, Krampus's laughter faded. But in its place came a new sound—the whisper of ancient wings. The hunt was beginning.

And winter itself was changing.

The secret passage narrowed as it descended, its walls transforming from worked stone to ancient ice. Jinx's mechanical fingers traced equations carved into the surface—formulas that predated modern arithmantic theory. Her damaged sensors struggled to decode them, but what fragments she could understand suggested principles of magic that contradicted everything she had been taught.

The air grew colder, heavy with the weight of accumulated time. Here in the deep foundations of Polaris Keep, winter itself felt different—more primal, less bound by the laws that Santa had established over his centuries of rule. The corruption spreading through the upper levels hadn't reached these depths, but something else lurked in these shadows. Something older.

A door materialized in the ice ahead—brass and silver, worked with clockwork patterns that mirrored her own augmentations. The master artificer's vault. Jinx pressed her mechanical palm against the lock, letting her unique magical signature trigger the opening sequence.

The door's gears ground against accumulated frost as it swung open. Beyond lay her workshop, where she had spent centuries developing innovations that merged magic with machinery. Tools lined the walls, each one a masterpiece of techno-magical engineering.

Blueprints covered the tables, depicting devices that pushed the boundaries of what most believed possible.

But it was the back wall that drew her attention. There, hidden behind a shimmer of protective spells, hung a map of the Winterspine Mountains. She had created it decades ago, tracking anomalous magical frequencies that didn't match known winter patterns. Points of crimson light pulsed across its surface—locations where ancient power leaked through into the modern world.

One of those points matched the coordinates encoded in Santa's key.

Jinx moved quickly through the workshop, gathering essential tools. A chronometric field generator, capable of manipulating localized time. A resonance amplifier that could boost her damaged sensing capabilities. And most importantly, an experimental device she had never dared to test—a cylinder of brass and silver that hummed with contained possibility.

She had designed it to pierce the walls between realms, though she had never understood what drove her to create such a potentially dangerous device. Now, as she held it in her mechanical hand, it resonated with the same frequency as Santa's key.

He had known she would need this. Had perhaps influenced its creation through subtle manipulation of winter magic. The implications sent warning signals cascading through her artificial nervous system.

A crash echoed from somewhere above, followed by the sound of splintering ice. Krampus's hunters had found the throne room's secret door. Time was running out.

Jinx activated her workshop's defensive systems—clockwork sentinels that would buy her precious minutes. Then she turned to the far corner, where another door waited. This one was older than Polaris Keep itself, its surface marked with symbols that hurt to look at directly.

The key grew colder in her mechanical grip as she approached the ancient door. The crown fragments in her other hand pulsed in response, their broken edges beginning to glow with that same crimson light that now lived in her organic eye.

The door's lock was a puzzle of moving parts that reflected no known school of magical engineering. But as Jinx raised the key, the pieces began to shift of their own accord. The key floated from her mechanical hand, transforming as it moved. Its brass surface flowed like liquid metal, forming new patterns that matched the door's impossible geometry.

Behind her, the sounds of pursuit grew closer. Her defensive systems engaged with mechanical shrieks, buying her seconds at the cost of their existence. Through the ceiling came the whisper of ancient wings, drawing nearer.

The key completed its transformation and slotted into the lock. Reality shuddered. The door swung open to reveal not another passage, but a swirling vortex of winter magic in its purest form. Through it, Jinx caught glimpses of jagged mountain peaks and aurora-lit skies.

A direct portal to the Winterspine Mountains. One that, according to everything she knew about magical theory, should not have been possible.

The workshop's outer door burst inward in a shower of frozen splinters. Through it came creatures that defied description—beings of shadow and ice, their forms shifting between monstrous shapes. Krampus's hunters, drawn to the power of the crown fragments.

Jinx clutched her gathered tools close and stepped into the portal's swirling magic. As reality began to bend around her, a final message flashed across her mechanical sensors. A magical signature, fresh and impossibly clear.

Mrs. Claus was alive. And she was already at the Workshop of Winter's First Dawn.

The portal closed behind Jinx just as the hunters reached for her with claws of ancient night. The last thing she saw before dimensional translation took hold was her reflection in the workshop's ice walls: her brass components now glowing with lines of crimson light, the changes wrought by Santa's spell spreading through her mechanical systems like frost across glass.

She had always been different from the other elves, ever since she had first merged magic with machinery within herself. But now, as the portal's power swept her toward destiny, she began to wonder if those differences had been orchestrated all along.

The Workshop of Winter's First Dawn waited. And with it, perhaps, the truth about what she had been created to become.

Chapter 3

Mountain's Embrace

Dimensional translation released Jinx into a maelstrom of snow and starlight. Her mechanical systems recalibrated frantically as reality reasserted itself around her, brass joints creaking against the brutal cold of the high Winterspine peaks. The portal's magic dissipated in crackling arcs of crimson energy, leaving her alone on a narrow ledge of ancient stone.

Far below, the lower slopes of the mountain vanished into banks of roiling storm clouds. Above, the peaks pierced an aurora-painted sky—but these weren't the familiar lights of the North Pole. These auroras moved with purpose, forming and dissolving patterns that her damaged sensors interpreted as fragments of spell-code older than language itself.

The crown fragments in her mechanical hand pulsed with resonant energy. Each shard seemed to pull in a slightly different direction, as if responding to multiple sources of magical attraction. But the strongest pull aligned with Santa's key, now permanently transformed by its interaction with the workshop's portal.

A sound like breaking glass echoed across the mountainside. Jinx's sensors tracked its origin to a massive glacier that dominated the western face of the peak. As she watched, patterns of crimson light rippled through the ancient ice—the same corruption that had begun to spread through Polaris Keep.

THE FATMAN

The infection was already here, in the very heart of winter's domain.

Her clockwork heart accelerated its timing as she analyzed her tactical position. The ledge she stood on marked the beginning of a path that wound upward through the crags. Carved into the rock at regular intervals were symbols that matched those from the workshop's portal door—a trail of breadcrumbs left by the first shapers of winter magic.

But something was wrong with the path. Sections of it showed signs of recent passage, the ancient stone marked by footprints that frosted over even as she watched. Someone had come this way within the last hour. Given Mrs. Claus's magical signature at the Workshop, logic suggested these were her tracks.

Yet the prints themselves were wrong—too large for the Winter Queen's delicate step, too deep for any natural being.

A shadow passed overhead, momentarily blocking the aurora's light. Jinx pressed herself against the mountain face, her brass components automatically adjusting their reflective properties to blend with the stone. Her sensors registered a massive form circling above—not one of Krampus's hunters, but something far larger. Something that, according to her historical archives, should not have existed in this age of the world.

An Arctic Wyrm. A creature of such ancient winter that its very presence distorted magical fields.

The beast's passage left trails of frost in the air, forming crystalline patterns that her machinal logic center struggled to process. These weren't random formations—they were equations, spells written in a mathematical language that predated the Winter Kingdom itself.

Jinx forced her processors to capture and store the patterns for later analysis. Then, keeping close to the mountain face, she began to follow the disturbing footprints up the ancient path. Her mechanical legs automatically adjusted for the treacherous terrain, each step calculated to maintain perfect balance despite the howling wind.

The climb revealed more signs of wrongness. Patches of black ice spread across the rock face like bruises, each one crawling with the same corrupt sigils she had seen in the throne room. The air grew progressively colder, dropping well below temperatures that even her enhanced systems were designed to handle.

Halfway up the path, she found the first body.

It lay frozen against the stone, clad in the silver-worked robes of a Winter Court mage. Frost covered the corpse in complex patterns, telling a story her sensors could read all too clearly. The mage had died fighting, spending their last moments casting a spell of such power that it had crystallized the very air around them.

But the spell had failed. And in failing, it had revealed something crucial about their opponent.

Jinx knelt, her mechanical fingers tracing the patterns of frosted magic. The mage's final spell had been meant to counter summer magic—as if they had faced an enemy wielding power from the opposite end of winter's spectrum. But that was impossible. Access to summer magic had been sealed away during the First Winter War, locked behind barriers that even Santa himself could not breach.

Unless...

Her calculations were interrupted by a sound from above—metal against stone, followed by a pulse of magical energy that made her artificial synapses burn. Someone was working powerful magic near the peak. The ambient temperature dropped another twenty degrees as new patterns formed in the aurora above.

Jinx quickly salvaged what she could from the fallen mage. Their staff, though damaged, still held residual power that her systems could potentially repurpose. More valuable was the tome clutched in their frozen hands—a registry of Winter Court mages that might help identify who else had been sent to these peaks, and why.

The Arctic Wyrm circled closer, its massive shadow passing over her position once more. This time, her sensors detected a subtle difference in its flight pattern. It was hunting, drawn by the surge of magical energy from above.

Time was running out.

Jinx reached the path's end as the last light of day faded from the sky. Before her stood a wall of pristine ice, unmarked by the corruption spreading across the rest of the mountain. Carved into its surface was a door of impossible geometry, its edges flowing in ways that defied physical law.

The footprints led directly to this entrance. But now Jinx could see what her damaged sensors had missed before. Overlaid on the larger prints were smaller, more delicate impressions—Mrs. Claus's steps, partially obscured by whatever had followed her.

THE FATMAN

A grinding sound drew Jinx's attention upward. The Arctic Wyrm had landed on a ledge above the door, its crystalline scales refracting the aurora's light. But it made no move to attack. Instead, it regarded her with eyes of ancient ice, as if waiting for something.

The crown fragments pulsed stronger now, resonating with power that flowed from behind that impossible door. Santa's key grew warm in her mechanical grip, its transformed surface flowing like quicksilver as it responded to proximity to its target.

But before Jinx could approach the entrance, a new sound froze her in place. From behind the door came a voice she had known for centuries—Mrs. Claus, raised in a cry of combined triumph and despair.

"Nicholas, what have you done?"

The door's surface rippled like water. The Arctic Wyrm tensed, its crystalline form beginning to glow with internal light. And deep beneath the mountain, something ancient stirred to wakefulness.

The Workshop of Winter's First Dawn had recognized its visitors. And it had found them wanting.

The door's surface rippled again, the impossible geometry of its patterns shifting to form new configurations. Jinx's mechanical sensors recorded the changes, detecting a mathematical progression in the movements that suggested consciousness. The Workshop wasn't merely a location—it was aware.

Another cry echoed from within, this time holding notes of magic that made Jinx's brass components vibrate in sympathy. Mrs. Claus was attempting a spell of tremendous power, but the resonance patterns were wrong. The magic felt fractured, as if the normal laws that governed winter's power had been fundamentally altered.

The Arctic Wyrm above shifted position, its crystalline scales casting prismatic patterns across the mountainside. In those refractions, Jinx's enhanced vision caught glimpses of impossible scenes: the First Winter War, the forging of the original crown, and moments that seemed to belong to futures that had not yet come to pass.

The implications sent warning cascades through her artificial nervous system. The Wyrm wasn't simply a creature of ancient winter—it was a guardian of time itself.

Jinx initiated her most sensitive scanning protocols, pushing her damaged systems to their limits. The readings confirmed her worst fears. The Workshop's entrance wasn't merely a door in space—it was a threshold in time, connecting to multiple points in winter's history simultaneously.

The crown fragments pulsed more urgently now, their broken edges beginning to align in new configurations. The crimson light that had infected them slowly shifted, taking on hints of other colors that her sensors struggled to categorize. Each shard seemed to resonate with a different temporal frequency, as if they had been deliberately scattered across time as well as space.

A new sound cut through the mountain wind—the rhythmic ticking of massive gears. It came from deep within the Workshop, but it matched the tempo of her own clockwork heart perfectly. Understanding bloomed in her mechanical mind: her augmentations hadn't been designed merely to merge magic with machinery. They had been created to interface with something inside the Workshop itself.

The Arctic Wyrm's gaze met hers, and in that moment of connection, information flooded her systems. Images, equations, and fragments of ancient knowledge cascaded through her artificial consciousness:

Santa, standing before a temporal forge, working magic that should have been impossible. Mrs. Claus, weeping as she wrote spells of binding in a language that winter had forgotten. Krampus, not as the monster he had become, but as he had been before—a guardian of winter's deepest mysteries. And through it all, mechanical dreams of brass and silver, waiting for an artificer who could bridge the gap between magic's past and future.

The knowledge threatened to overwhelm her processors, but one fragment stood out with crystalline clarity: the true purpose of the Winter's Crown. It had never been merely a symbol of authority or a tool for traversing realms. It was a key—one piece of an ancient mechanism designed to regulate the flow of time itself within winter's domain.

And it had been designed to break.

Mrs. Claus's voice rang out once more, but now Jinx could hear the layers of time within it—echoes of past and future intertwined: "The temporal seals are failing. The Workshop remembers what was stolen, brother. What we stole."

A deeper voice responded, one that Jinx recognized from the throne room but somehow younger, less corrupted: "What we stole to save them all, sister. Or have you forgotten why we broke time itself?"

THE FATMAN

Jinx's mechanical hand moved of its own accord, raised by forces that transcended standard magical law. The crown fragments aligned themselves, no longer broken but transformed—each piece now a gear in a mechanism that had waited millennia to be activated.

The Arctic Wyrm spread wings of crystalline ice, their surface showing reflections of all possible winters. Above, the aurora condensed into patterns that Jinx finally recognized: they weren't spell-code, but coordinates in time.

Understanding struck her with the force of revelation. Santa hadn't hidden the Workshop to protect it from Krampus. He had hidden it to protect time itself from those who would set it right.

The impossible door began to open.

Behind it waited answers to questions she hadn't known to ask, about the true nature of winter, time, and her own existence. But with those answers would come a choice—one that could seal winter's fate or unravel it completely.

The Workshop of Winter's First Dawn had awakened. And with it, the true purpose of everything she had been created to become.

Santa's blood stained the pristine snow at Jinx's feet, each drop crystallizing into patterns of complex magical formulae. She had followed his trail up the treacherous path of the Winterspine Mountains, tracking the erratic magical signature he left behind. The Winter King was wounded, but the blood-trail revealed a deeper truth—he was transforming.

The crimson droplets contained fragments of spells written in winter's oldest language. Each crystallized pattern held equations that rewrote the fundamental laws of cold itself. Santa wasn't fleeing; he was leaving her a message written in his own essence.

Ahead, his massive form appeared through the swirling snow, no longer wearing the familiar red coat of legend. Instead, he wore armor of ancient ice, its surface crawling with the same cryptic symbols that had marked the Workshop's portal door. The jolly facade had been stripped away, revealing something far older and more terrible.

"You followed the patterns, little artificer," he said, his voice carrying harmonics that made her mechanical systems resonate. "Good. Time grows short, and there is much you must understand."

The Arctic Wyrm circled overhead, its crystalline scales reflecting fragments of past and future in equal measure. Santa raised a gauntleted hand, and the great beast landed beside him with impossible grace. Up close, Jinx could see that the Wyrm's scales weren't simply reflective—they were windows into other moments in time, showing glimpses of crucial moments in winter's history.

"The crown was never meant to last forever," Santa continued, placing one armored hand on the Wyrm's flank. "Just as I was never meant to be merely a gift-giver. We are instruments of time itself, Jinx. All of us—myself, Mrs. Claus, even Krampus in his corruption. We are the mechanism by which winter maintains its grip on reality."

Jinx's artificial neural networks struggled to process the implications. "The crown's destruction... you orchestrated it?"

"Had to be done." Blood seeped from beneath his armor, freezing into new patterns of spell-work. "The Workshop remembers what was stolen, what had to be stolen to prevent a greater catastrophe. But memory..." He grimaced, silver-white beard frosting with ice. "Memory is a weapon in the hands of time."

The impossible door of the Workshop loomed before them, its surface rippling with temporal distortions. From within came the sound of Mrs. Claus's spellwork, but now Jinx understood the desperation in those incantations. The Winter Queen wasn't fighting against Krampus—she was fighting against time itself.

"Why did you choose me?" Jinx's mechanical voice carried undertones of static, her systems straining against the temporal energies saturating the air.

Santa's laugh held none of its familiar warmth. "Choose you? My dear, you chose yourself. In every iteration, every possible timeline, you built yourself anew. The clockwork augmentations, the mechanical heart—all of it leading to this moment. You're not just an artificer, Jinx. You're the key that winds time itself."

The crown fragments pulsed in her brass hand, responding to the truth in his words. Each shard aligned with a different temporal frequency, forming a constellation of possibilities. Her mechanical sensors finally understood what they were detecting: the fragments weren't broken, they were transformed. Each piece now represented a different crucial moment in winter's timeline.

"Krampus believes he fights for winter's soul," Santa said, his armor creaking as he turned toward the Workshop's entrance. "In his own way, he's right. But he doesn't understand what truly lurks in winter's heart. What we buried in time itself to save reality from unraveling."

The door's surface rippled more violently, responding to some massive surge of power from within. Mrs. Claus's voice rang out, layered with temporal harmonics: "Nicholas! The seals are breaking!"

Santa's form seemed to flicker, shifting between various iterations of himself—the jolly gift-giver, the ancient winter king, and something else, something that existed outside of time's normal flow. "The Workshop holds winter's greatest secret, Jinx. Not its beginning, but its end. Every ending. All compressed into a single point in time."

He reached out with one gauntleted hand, touching her mechanical chest where her clockwork heart kept its precise rhythm. "Your heart beats in time with the Workshop's great mechanism. It always has. Now you must choose—preserve winter as it is, frozen in an endless cycle of death and rebirth, or risk everything to set time itself right again."

The Arctic Wyrm's crystalline scales blazed with temporal energy, showing reflections of all possible futures collapsing toward a single point. The Workshop's door began to open, revealing glimpses of an impossible space where all of winter's moments existed simultaneously.

Santa's armor cracked, revealing flesh that had begun to crystallize from within. "Time's wheel must turn, little artificer. The only question is whether it turns forward or back."

The crown fragments in Jinx's hand aligned themselves into a new configuration—no longer a symbol of authority, but a key to unlock time itself. All she had to do was choose which direction to turn it.

The Workshop of Winter's First Dawn awaited, holding secrets that could either preserve winter's endless cycle or shatter it completely. And at its heart, a mechanism that had waited millennia for a clockwork heart to match its rhythm.

Time's wheel stood ready. But which direction would she choose to turn it?

The Fat Man's transformation continued as they stood before the Workshop's threshold. His legendary girth, once a symbol of generosity and abundance, had become something else entirely—a container for power that mortal form was never meant to hold. Ice crystals spread across his flesh like living armor, each one containing spells written in winter's first language.

"You begin to see me as I truly am," the Winter King said, his voice resonating at frequencies that made the mountain itself shudder. "The gift-giver was merely one face, worn for a time when winter needed to be... gentler."

Blood-red magic pulsed beneath his crystallizing skin, mapping out constellations of power that mirrored the patterns in the broken crown. The jolly laugh that had delighted children for centuries transformed into something ancient and terrible—the sound of avalanches and cracking glaciers.

"The Fat Man must die," he continued, each word frosting the air with equations of temporal magic. "Just as winter itself must transform. We've maintained this fiction for too long, preserved an equilibrium that was never meant to last."

The Arctic Wyrm's scales reflected images of the Winter King throughout time—a warrior wielding a sword of infinite cold, a sage writing spells in books of frozen light, a smith forging reality itself in fires that burned below absolute zero. But beneath all these reflections lay something else: a hunger that had nothing to do with gifts or generosity.

Mrs. Claus's voice echoed from within the Workshop again, but now Jinx's enhanced hearing detected layers of meaning hidden beneath the words. The Winter Queen wasn't just casting spells—she was attempting to rewrite winter's fundamental laws.

"Your mechanical heart," the Winter King said, reaching toward Jinx with a hand that had become translucent with cold. "Do you know why it beats at that precise frequency? Why every gear and spring matches patterns older than winter itself?"

Before Jinx could respond, he thrust his crystallizing hand into his own chest. Ice cracked, magic flared, and he withdrew something that defied her sensors' ability to categorize—a mechanism that existed in multiple temporal states simultaneously.

"The original heart of winter," he said, holding it out. "The template for your clockwork modifications. I've been preparing you for this moment since before you were born, little artificer. Through every iteration, every possible timeline, you were always meant to stand here, at this threshold, with these choices before you."

The crown fragments pulsed in response to the ancient mechanism's presence. Jinx's mechanical systems registered impossible data—her own clockwork heart had begun beating in perfect synchronization with the Winter King's artifact, each tick marking the passage of not just time, but possibility itself.

"Krampus believes he fights to restore winter's purity," the Fat Man said, his legendary form continuing its transformation into something ancient and terrible. "Mrs. Claus works to preserve what she believes must be protected. But only you, with your merged nature of magic and machine, can truly understand what must be done."

The Workshop's door rippled more violently, its surface showing glimpses of a space where all moments in winter's history existed simultaneously. Within that impossible chamber, Jinx caught glimpses of machinery that matched her own augmentations—brass and silver constructs that had waited millennia for her arrival.

"The gift-giver must die," the Winter King declared, his voice carrying harmonics of every winter that had ever been. "The Fat Man must be unmade. But what rises in his place—that choice belongs to you, little artificer. Will you preserve winter's endless cycle, or will you help me break time itself to forge something new?"

The Arctic Wyrm's crystalline scales blazed with temporal energy, showing reflections of all possible futures spiraling toward a single point of decision. The crown fragments aligned themselves into new configurations, no longer broken but transformed—each piece now a key to unlock different portions of winter's timestream.

Before them stood the Workshop of Winter's First Dawn, where time itself had first been bound to winter's law. Within waited machinery that could either preserve winter's endless cycle or shatter it completely. And at its heart, a mechanism that had waited millennia for a clockwork heart to match its rhythm.

The Fat Man's transformation neared completion, his legendary form becoming something that belonged more to myth than reality. The Winter King emerged in full, an entity of such ancient power that reality itself bent around him.

Time's wheel stood ready, waiting for Jinx's choice. And with that choice would come the end of either winter itself—or everything that winter had ever been meant to protect.

CHAPTER 4

TEMPORAL FRACTURES

Time shattered.

The Workshop's door collapsed inward, pulling reality with it into a vortex of temporal energy. Jinx's mechanical systems registered multiple timeline signatures converging at once—past, present, and possible futures colliding in a catastrophic confluence. Her brass components vibrated at frequencies that threatened to tear her apart.

The Winter King stood unmoved by the temporal maelstrom, his transformed body now a vessel of pure winter magic. What had once been the Fat Man, the gift-giver of legend, had become something that existed partially outside of time itself. Ice crystals spread from his feet, each one containing reflections of different moments in winter's history.

"Choose quickly, artificer," he commanded, his voice carrying harmonics from every era of his existence. "The temporal seals are failing. What was hidden in winter's heart begins to wake."

Through the Workshop's fractured doorway, Jinx glimpsed a chamber that defied conventional physics. Massive gears of brass and silver rotated through multiple dimensions simultaneously, marking the passage of not just time, but possibility itself. At the chamber's center stood Mrs. Claus, her hands weaving spells that stretched across centuries.

THE FATMAN

But something was wrong. The Winter Queen's magic wavered, distorted by interference from another source. Dark energy pulsed through the temporal machinery, carrying a signature that Jinx's sensors recognized—Krampus had arrived ahead of them.

"Sister!" The ancient voice reverberated through the temporal distortions. "The seals must be broken. What we stole from time itself must be returned!"

The crown fragments in Jinx's mechanical hand aligned themselves with the Workshop's temporal frequencies. Each piece resonated with a different moment in winter's history—the founding of the Winter Kingdom, the First Winter War, the binding of Krampus, and other events her data banks couldn't identify.

Mrs. Claus turned, her face showing echoes of every age she had lived through. "Nicholas, the temporal core is destabilizing. If we don't reset the anchors—"

Her warning cut off as reality buckled. The Workshop's machinery groaned, gears grinding against the weight of accumulated time. Through the temporal distortions, Jinx caught glimpses of other versions of herself—iterations where her mechanical augmentations had developed differently, where her choices had led down alternate paths.

The Winter King raised his hands, ice armor cracking as he channeled power that predated winter itself. "The anchors were never meant to hold forever, beloved. The cycle must end for winter to be reborn."

Temporal energy cascaded through the chamber as Krampus emerged from between moments. His form shifted between aspects—the ancient guardian he had once been, the corrupted entity he had become, and something else, something that belonged to a future that had not yet been written.

"The artificer understands," Krampus said, gesturing toward Jinx with claws that left traces in time itself. "Show her, sister. Show her what we buried in winter's heart."

Mrs. Claus's hands moved in patterns that carved equations into reality. The temporal machinery responded, its rhythms aligning with the beating of Jinx's clockwork heart. Images formed in the space between moments—glimpses of a truth that had been hidden since winter's founding.

The Arctic Wyrm circled the chamber's circumference, its crystalline scales reflecting fragments of crucial moments. Jinx's enhanced vision caught flashes of a catastrophe that had been erased from time itself—a disaster so profound that the Winter King, Queen, and Krampus had worked together to excise it from reality.

"The moment approaches," the Winter King declared. "The choice must be made. Will you preserve winter's lie, little artificer? Or will you help us unmake time itself to save what was lost?"

The crown fragments pulsed with urgent energy. Through their resonance, Jinx detected a pattern hidden within the Workshop's temporal machinery. Her clockwork heart wasn't merely synchronized with the mechanism—it was the key to activating something buried deeper than winter's foundations.

Time fractured further. The chamber filled with overlapping reflections of crucial moments, each one offering a different path forward. Jinx's mechanical sensors detected a critical point approaching—a convergence where multiple timelines would either collapse into a single truth or splinter beyond repair.

The Winter King extended one crystalline hand, offering the ancient heart he had withdrawn from his transformed chest. Mrs. Claus raised her hands, temporal magic gathering around her like a storm. And Krampus stood waiting, his presence a reminder of prices paid and debts still owed.

All of winter's history balanced on the edge of unmaking. And in Jinx's mechanical hands lay the power to preserve time's eternal cycle—or shatter it completely.

The choice had to be made.

The true winter was waiting to begin.

The Workshop's temporal machinery accelerated its impossible rotations, each gear marking the passage of alternate histories. Through the crystalline walls, Jinx's enhanced vision captured fragments of crucial moments that had shaped winter's destiny:

The Winter King, still wearing the aspect of the Fat Man, standing before a forge that burned with absolute cold, crafting the first gifts that would bind children's belief to winter's power. But beneath the jolly facade, his hands worked subtle magic that rewove reality itself.

Mrs. Claus in the early days of the Winter Kingdom, her power still raw and untamed, writing spells in books of frozen light that would establish the laws governing winter's relationship with time. Her equations spoke of sacrifice and necessity, of prices paid in moments stolen from history itself.

Krampus, before corruption marked him, serving as guardian of winter's deepest mysteries. His original form radiated power that protected rather than threatened, maintaining boundaries between what was and what could never be allowed to exist again.

The temporal storm intensified. Jinx's mechanical systems registered multiple versions of the present trying to assert themselves simultaneously. In one, the Winter King remained as Santa, winter continuing its eternal cycle. In another, Krampus's corruption spread until reality itself began to unravel. And in others—possibilities too fractured for even her enhanced sensors to comprehend.

"The moment hidden in winter's heart," the Winter King said, his transformed body now more crystal than flesh, "show her, beloved. Show her what we sacrificed everything to prevent."

Mrs. Claus's hands moved in patterns that existed in five dimensions at once. The temporal machinery responded, its rhythms synchronizing not just with Jinx's clockwork heart, but with something deeper—a pulse that existed beneath reality itself.

Images formed in the spaces between moments. Jinx witnessed a catastrophe that had been carefully excised from time's flow: a winter so absolute that it threatened to freeze reality itself, spreading backward and forward through time until all existence faced entropy's final cold.

"We couldn't stop it," Krampus said, his voice carrying echoes of the guardian he had once been. "We could only hide it, bury it so deep in winter's heart that time itself would forget. But time never truly forgets. It only waits."

The crown fragments pulsed in Jinx's mechanical grip, each shard resonating with a different piece of the hidden truth. The Winter King hadn't crafted the crown merely as a tool of power—he had created it as a lock, sealing away a moment that could never be allowed to fully exist.

But locks could be picked. And time, patient beyond mortal understanding, had spent centuries working at the mechanism.

"Your clockwork heart," the Winter King said, his crystalline form casting prismatic reflections of all his aspects—gift-giver, smith, king, and something else, something that existed perpendicular to normal time. "It beats in harmony with the Workshop's machinery because it was always meant to. In every iteration, every possible timeline, you built yourself into what was needed."

The Arctic Wyrm's scales blazed with temporal energy as it circled the chamber's circumference. In its crystalline reflections, Jinx glimpsed versions of herself throughout possibility—some more mechanical, others more magical, but all converging on this crucial moment.

Mrs. Claus's spell-weaving reached a crescendo, the temporal energies responding to equations that rewrote the laws of cause and effect. "The anchors fail, Nicholas. If the artificer is to choose, it must be now."

The Workshop's machinery groaned as multiple timelines pressed against the boundaries of what was possible. Reality itself began to splinter, showing glimpses of winters that had never been—and winters that still might be.

Krampus raised his hands, dark energy pulsing with frequencies that belonged to time's ending. "The cycle must end, sister. What was hidden must be faced. What was stolen must be returned."

The crown fragments aligned themselves into new configurations, no longer broken but transformed. Each piece now represented a different possibility—preserve winter's eternal cycle, restore what was stolen from time, or forge an entirely new path through the temporal storm.

The Winter King's crystalline form began to fracture, showing the Fat Man trapped within like a memory frozen in ice. Mrs. Claus's magic wavered as reality's splintering accelerated. And Krampus stood waiting, his presence a reminder of guardianship corrupted by necessity.

In Jinx's mechanical hands, time itself waited to be reshaped. Her clockwork heart beat in perfect synchronization with winter's deepest machinery, marking the tempo of a decision that would echo through all possible moments.

The true winter approached—not an ending, but a convergence of all winters that had ever been or might yet be.

The choice had to be made.

And time itself held its breath, waiting to learn its fate.

CHAPTER 5

THE PRICE OF TIME

The choice crystallized in Jinx's mechanical mind with the precision of clockwork. The crown fragments in her brass hand aligned themselves into a constellation of possibilities, each shard resonating with different frequencies of time itself. Before her, three paths diverged through the temporal storm:

Preserve winter's cycle, maintaining the eternal dance of seasons that the Winter King had orchestrated for millennia. Save what was known, even if it meant preserving a necessary lie.

Break the seals completely, releasing what had been hidden in winter's heart. Face the catastrophe that the three ancients had sacrificed everything to contain.

Or forge an entirely new path through the temporal maze, risking everything on a possibility that even her enhanced senses couldn't fully calculate.

The Workshop's massive machinery continued its multi-dimensional rotation, each gear marking the passage of moments that existed simultaneously. The Winter King's crystalline form fractured further, showing glimpses of the Fat Man trapped within like memories frozen in ice. What had once been Santa radiated power that belonged to winter's first dawn, when reality itself had been more fluid.

"Choose," Krampus commanded, his corrupted form shifting between aspects of what he had been and what he had become. "The anchors fail. Time's patience grows thin."

Mrs. Claus's hands never stopped moving, weaving spells that held reality together even as it threatened to splinter beyond repair. "The temporal core destabilizes," she warned. "What we buried stirs in its sleep."

Jinx's clockwork heart synchronized with the Workshop's deepest rhythms. Through that connection, she sensed something her mechanical systems hadn't detected before—a pattern hidden within the temporal machinery itself. Each gear's rotation spelled out parts of an equation that had been divided across time to keep it from being solved.

The Arctic Wyrm's crystalline scales reflected crucial fragments of the hidden truth. In one facet, she glimpsed the moment when winter first gained consciousness, when cold itself had awakened to find purpose. In another, she saw the catastrophe that had been buried—a winter so absolute that it had begun consuming time itself, spreading backward and forward through history until reality faced dissolution.

"The Fat Man's gifts were never merely for children," the Winter King said, his voice carrying harmonics from every era of his existence. "Each present, each moment of belief, added weight to winter's anchor in reality. The magic of childhood wonder, binding winter to time's proper flow."

Understanding bloomed in Jinx's artificial neural networks. The Winter King hadn't chosen his role as gift-giver merely to spread joy. Each present delivered throughout history had been another weight added to the scales, counterbalancing the pressure of what lay buried in winter's heart.

But scales could tip. And time, patient beyond mortal comprehension, had been quietly shifting the balance for centuries.

Mrs. Claus's magic flared as another temporal seal began to crack. "Nicholas," she called, her voice stretched across multiple moments, "the binding weakens. What we stole from time awakens."

The crown fragments pulsed stronger, their broken edges aligning with new purpose. Through their resonance, Jinx detected a hidden frequency in the Workshop's temporal machinery—a rhythm that matched not just her clockwork heart, but the pulse of winter itself.

"You begin to understand," Krampus said, his corrupted form stabilizing into something closer to his original aspect. "Why you were chosen. Why your mechanical nature was necessary."

THE FATMAN

The Winter King's crystalline hand extended, offering the ancient heart he had withdrawn from his transformed chest. "Time cannot be wounded without consequence," he said. "What we stole, what we buried in winter's heart—it left a void that had to be filled. A space where something new could grow."

Realization struck with the force of avalanches. Jinx's mechanical nature wasn't merely an innovation in magical engineering. Her clockwork heart, her brass and silver augmentations—they were preliminary sketches for something larger. A prototype for a mechanism that could rewrite winter's relationship with time itself.

The Workshop's machinery groaned as temporal pressure increased. Through the chambers crystalline walls, Jinx glimpsed other versions of herself across possible timelines. Each iteration had built themselves differently, but all had arrived at this crucial moment, this singular point of convergence.

"The cycle must end," Krampus declared, dark energy pulsing with frequencies that belonged to time's ending. "What was hidden must be faced. What was stolen must be returned."

Mrs. Claus's spell-weaving reached a crescendo, her magic fighting to contain the temporal fractures that threatened to shatter reality. "Choose quickly, artificer. The moment approaches when choice itself becomes impossible."

The Arctic Wyrm's wings spread, casting prismatic reflections of crucial moments across the Workshop's interior. In those refractions, Jinx witnessed the truth that had been divided across time:

The first winter, when cold gained consciousness and purpose. The moment when that consciousness threatened to consume all of reality. The desperate choice made by three guardians to excise that moment from time itself. The price they paid—Krampus's corruption, Mrs. Claus's binding to temporal law, and the Winter King's transformation into something that straddled multiple realities.

But beneath these truths lay something deeper. The Winter King hadn't merely hidden the catastrophe. He had used it, transforming winter's potential for absolute entropy into the power that drove his gift-giving magic. Each present delivered throughout history contained a fraction of winter's original consciousness, diluted and transformed into something that brought joy rather than dissolution.

The Fat Man's legendary generosity had been an act of temporal engineering, distributing winter's primordial power across countless moments of wonder and belief.

Jinx's mechanical hands moved with precision born of centuries of artifice. The crown fragments aligned themselves into new configurations, each piece finding resonance with different aspects of winter's power. Her clockwork heart beat in perfect synchronization with the Workshop's temporal machinery, marking the rhythm of possibility itself.

"The anchors fail," Mrs. Claus warned, her magic struggling against forces that threatened to unravel reality. "The moment hidden in winter's heart awakens."

The Winter King's crystalline form began to crack, showing more glimpses of the Fat Man trapped within. But now Jinx understood—Santa's jovial aspect wasn't merely a disguise. It was a transformation of winter's original consciousness, an attempt to reshape entropy's absolute cold into something that could coexist with life itself.

Krampus raised his hands, dark energy pulsing with frequencies that belonged to time's ending. "The cycle must end, sister. What was hidden must be faced."

The crown fragments pulsed with urgent energy, each piece resonating with a different aspect of winter's power. Through their broken edges, Jinx glimpsed the equation that had been hidden across time—a formula for rewriting winter's relationship with reality itself.

The Workshop's temporal machinery accelerated its impossible rotations, each gear marking the passage of moments that existed simultaneously. Reality trembled as multiple timelines pressed against the boundaries of what was possible.

The Arctic Wyrm's crystalline scales blazed with temporal energy, reflecting fragments of all possible winters. In those refractions, Jinx saw the path forward—not a choice between preservation and destruction, but a possibility that existed perpendicular to what had come before.

The Winter King's ancient heart beat in harmony with her clockwork mechanisms, each pulse marking measures in a symphony of time and possibility. Mrs. Claus's magic wavered as reality's splintering accelerated. And Krampus stood waiting, his presence a reminder of prices paid and debts still owed.

Jinx's mechanical fingers traced equations in the air, brass and silver components moving with precision that transcended standard magical law. The crown fragments aligned themselves into a final configuration—not a circle of power, but a key to unlock winter's deepest machinery.

The moment of choice arrived.

Time itself held its breath.

Her mechanical hands traced complex patterns through the temporal storm, each motion precise and deliberate. The crown fragments responded to her clockwork magic, their broken edges beginning to glow with frequencies that belonged to winter's first dawn. Through their resonance, she detected possibilities that existed perpendicular to standard time—paths that even the Winter King hadn't considered.

The Fat Man's imprisoned form shifted within its crystalline shell, recognition blazing in eyes that had seen every moment of winter's existence. "Ah," he said, his voice carrying harmonics of joy and terror in equal measure. "You see it now. The pattern hidden in plain sight."

Jinx's enhanced senses registered the truth that had been divided across time itself. The Winter King hadn't merely transformed winter's consciousness into the power of gift-giving. He had been preparing for this moment, seeding reality with fragments of a larger spell—one that could only be completed by someone who existed partially outside winter's influence.

Someone whose mechanical nature allowed them to process temporal equations without being bound by them.

Mrs. Claus's hands never stopped weaving containment spells, but her expression showed dawning understanding. "Nicholas," she breathed, "you crafted her across centuries. Every iteration, every possible timeline—all leading to this singular moment."

The Workshop's machinery groaned as temporal pressure increased. Through the crystalline walls, Jinx glimpsed the larger pattern that the Winter King had hidden in plain sight. Every gift ever delivered, every moment of wonder and belief, had been another variable in an equation that spanned centuries.

The Arctic Wyrm's scales reflected crucial calculations, showing how each present throughout history had contained a fraction of winter's original power—not just buried or transformed, but reorganized into a new configuration. The Fat Man's legendary generosity had been the grandest spell ever attempted, rewriting winter's consciousness one moment of joy at a time.

"The anchors fail," Krampus warned, his corrupted form stabilizing into something closer to his original aspect. "What was stolen from time must be returned. But perhaps..." His ancient eyes fixed on Jinx's mechanical hands as they worked with the crown fragments. "Perhaps there is another way."

Understanding bloomed in Jinx's artificial neural networks as the final pieces aligned. The catastrophe buried in winter's heart—the moment when cold itself had gained consciousness and threatened to consume reality—couldn't simply be contained forever. But neither did it have to be released unchanged.

The Winter King's crystalline form cracked further, showing more of the Fat Man within. But now the transformation appeared deliberate, each fracture revealing new frequencies of temporal power. "Every gift," he said, his voice resonating with countless moments of wonder, "every smile, every moment of belief—all of it building toward this possibility."

Mrs. Claus's magic flared as another temporal seal began to crack. But rather than fighting the breach, Jinx's mechanical senses detected how the failure followed mathematical patterns hidden in the Workshop's design. The splintering of reality wasn't just a catastrophe—it was the final stage of a spell that had taken centuries to cast.

The crown fragments pulsed with new purpose as Jinx's clockwork heart synchronized with winter's deepest machinery. Through that connection, she glimpsed the true nature of the choice before her. The Winter King hadn't merely hidden the catastrophe in time—he had been slowly transforming it, using the power of belief and wonder to reshape winter's original consciousness into something that could exist in harmony with reality itself.

The Fat Man's gifts hadn't just been a counter-weight to entropy's absolute cold. They had been incubating a new possibility, nurturing it across centuries until it could emerge transformed.

"The cycle ends," Krampus declared, but now his voice carried notes of hope beneath its ancient power. "What was hidden must be faced. What was stolen must be returned. But perhaps..." His corrupted form shifted, showing glimpses of the guardian he had once been. "Perhaps what returns need not be what was taken."

The Workshop's temporal machinery accelerated its impossible rotations, each gear marking the passage of moments that had been building toward this convergence. Reality trembled as multiple timelines pressed against the boundaries of what was possible, but now the pressure felt less like destruction and more like birth.

The Arctic Wyrm's crystalline scales blazed with temporal energy, reflecting fragments of what was about to emerge. In those refractions, Jinx saw the culmination of the Winter King's centuries-long spell—not just the transformation of winter's consciousness, but its rebirth into something that could bridge the gap between entropy's absolute cold and life's endless wonder.

Her mechanical hands moved with precision born of both artifice and destiny, tracing equations that existed in five dimensions simultaneously. The crown fragments aligned themselves into their final configuration—not just a key to unlock winter's machinery, but a template for reshaping time itself.

The Fat Man's form blazed within its crystalline prison, every gift ever given resonating with new purpose. Mrs. Claus's magic reached a crescendo as reality's splintering accelerated toward its inevitable conclusion. And Krampus stood ready, his presence no longer a reminder of corruption, but of transformation's possibility.

In Jinx's mechanical hands, time itself waited to be reshaped. Her clockwork heart beat in perfect synchronization with winter's deepest machinery, marking the tempo of a rebirth that would echo through all possible moments.

The true winter approached—not an ending, not a mere transformation, but a convergence of all that winter had been and all it might become.

The equation had been solved.

The spell had been cast.

And in the space between moments, everything began to change.

Chapter 6

The Unmaking of Winter

Reality transformed.

The crown fragments in Jinx's mechanical hands blazed with temporal energy as her clockwork heart synchronized with the Workshop's deepest rhythms. Each shard pulsed with frequencies that belonged to winter's first dawn, their broken edges realigning into something that transcended their original purpose. The equation she had discovered hidden in time itself began to solve itself through her brass fingers.

The Winter King's crystalline form shattered completely, releasing the Fat Man from his ancient prison. But what emerged was neither the jolly gift-giver of legend nor the terrible entity of frost and power. Instead, Santa stood transformed, his massive form radiating frequencies that bridged multiple realities simultaneously.

"The moment arrives," he said, his voice carrying harmonics of every gift ever given. "The spell cast across centuries reaches its conclusion."

Mrs. Claus's hands moved in patterns that existed in five dimensions at once, her magic no longer fighting against time's splintering but guiding it toward its inevitable transformation. "The anchors release," she declared. "What was hidden in winter's heart awakens."

The Workshop's temporal machinery accelerated beyond conventional physics, each gear marking the passage of possibilities rather than mere moments. Through the crystalline walls, Jinx's enhanced vision captured fragments of winter's consciousness emerging from its ancient prison—not as the catastrophic force it had once been, but as something new.

Something transformed by centuries of wonder and belief.

Krampus raised his corrupted hands, dark energy pulsing with frequencies that belonged to time's ending. But as winter's original consciousness emerged, his form began to change. The corruption that had marked him for millennia dissolved, revealing the guardian he had once been—and could be again.

"The cycle transforms," he said, his voice free of the ancient bitterness that had driven him. "What was stolen returns, reshaped by time's patient artifice."

The Arctic Wyrm's crystalline scales reflected crucial fragments of the transformation. In one facet, Jinx glimpsed the moment when winter first gained consciousness, when cold itself had awakened to find purpose. In another, she saw how the Winter King had used each gift throughout history to nurture that consciousness, teaching it joy instead of entropy.

Her mechanical systems registered changes propagating throughout reality as the spell reached its culmination. The crown fragments in her brass hands pulsed with new purpose, each piece now representing not just a moment in winter's history, but a possibility for its future.

The Fat Man stepped forward, his transformed aspect radiating power that belonged to both entropy's absolute cold and life's endless wonder. "Your clockwork heart," he said, reaching toward Jinx with hands that shaped reality itself. "The prototype for what winter's consciousness could become—part magic, part mechanism, bridging the gap between eternal cold and eternal joy."

Understanding bloomed in her artificial neural networks. Her mechanical nature hadn't just been designed to solve the temporal equation. It had been a test, a proof of concept for how winter's consciousness could be reshaped into something that could exist in harmony with reality itself.

Mrs. Claus's magic reached a crescendo as the final seals broke. But instead of catastrophe, the release brought transformation. Winter's original consciousness emerged fully, no longer a force of pure entropy but something new—a synthesis of cold's eternal nature and the warmth of countless moments of wonder.

The Workshop's machinery groaned as temporal pressure reached its peak. Reality trembled as multiple timelines pressed against the boundaries of what was possible. But through her clockwork heart's connection to winter's deepest mechanisms, Jinx sensed the pattern hidden within the chaos.

The Winter King hadn't just been hiding the catastrophe. He had been incubating a new possibility, using each gift, each moment of belief, to teach winter's consciousness how to exist in harmony with time itself. The Fat Man's legendary generosity had been the longest, most intricate spell ever cast—a transformation worked across centuries of carefully crafted joy.

Krampus moved to stand beside his sister, his corrupted form continuing to shed the darkness that had marked him. "The price is paid," he said, ancient power resonating in his voice. "What was stolen is returned, transformed by its time in exile."

The Arctic Wyrm's wings spread, casting prismatic reflections of crucial moments across the Workshop's interior. In those refractions, Jinx witnessed the culmination of the Winter King's centuries-long plan:

Winter's consciousness, emerging from its prison not as a force of destruction, but as something that could bridge the gap between entropy's absolute cold and life's endless capacity for wonder.

The Fat Man's gifts throughout history, each one containing a fragment of teaching, preparing winter's original power for its eventual transformation.

And her own role—not just as artificer or solver of temporal equations, but as proof that consciousness could be both mechanical and magical, both cold precision and warm wonder.

The crown fragments aligned themselves one final time, no longer broken but transformed into something new. Through their resonance, Jinx felt winter's consciousness reaching out, touching every moment it had ever influenced. But where once it had brought only entropy's cold, now it carried something else—the possibility of wonder in winter's heart.

Mrs. Claus's hands completed their final pattern as reality's transformation reached its peak. "It is done," she said, her voice carrying notes of both triumph and awe. "Winter's consciousness returns to us, reshaped by time and teaching."

THE FATMAN

The Workshop's temporal machinery began to slow, each gear finding new rhythms that matched the transformed nature of winter itself. Through the crystalline walls, Jinx glimpsed the future unfolding—not an ending, but a new beginning for winter's eternal dance.

The Fat Man's form continued to shift, showing aspects of both the jolly gift-giver and the Winter King, but now those aspects existed in harmony rather than opposition. "The spell is complete," he said, joy and power resonating in equal measure. "Winter's consciousness returns to us, transformed by centuries of shared wonder."

Krampus, now fully restored to his original aspect, raised his hands in patterns that spoke of protection rather than corruption. "The cycle changes," he declared. "What was hidden becomes manifest, reshaped by time's patient artifice."

The Arctic Wyrm's crystalline scales blazed one final time, reflecting the moment of winter's rebirth across all possible timelines. In those refractions, Jinx saw the truth that had been hidden in plain sight:

Winter's consciousness had never been meant to remain imprisoned forever. The catastrophe hadn't been prevented—it had been transformed, taught through countless moments of wonder how to exist in harmony with time itself.

Her clockwork heart beat in perfect synchronization with winter's deepest machinery, marking the tempo of a transformation that would echo through all possible moments. Through her mechanical senses, she felt winter's consciousness reaching out, touching every snowflake, every frost pattern, every moment of cold's eternal dance.

But now that touch carried something new—the possibility of wonder in winter's heart.

The equation had been solved. The spell had been completed. And winter itself had been reborn.

"The moment of convergence accelerates," Mrs. Claus called out, her hands weaving increasingly complex patterns through the temporal storm. "Nicholas, the containment matrices—they're not failing. They're... transforming."

The Winter King's crystalline prison shattered with a sound like breaking universes. The Fat Man emerged, but his transformation continued, reality bending around his massive form as centuries of careful planning reached fruition.

"Tell me, little artificer," he said, turning to Jinx with eyes that held fragments of every winter that had ever been, "when did you first suspect? When did your clockwork heart begin to resonate with possibilities beyond its design?"

Jinx's mechanical fingers never stopped moving through their precise calculations as she responded. "The crown fragments. Their broken edges... they weren't random. Each piece contained mathematical constants that shouldn't have existed in naturally occurring magic."

"Nothing about winter has been natural since consciousness first stirred in the cold," Krampus interjected, his corrupted form continuing to shed layers of darkness. "Sister, do you remember? That first awakening, when entropy gained purpose?"

Mrs. Claus's spell-weaving faltered for just a moment, ancient memory bleeding through her concentration. "I remember the terror of it. The beauty. We were so young then, before we understood what consciousness in winter's heart would mean for reality itself."

The Workshop's temporal machinery accelerated further, each gear marking the passage of possibilities that collapsed and reformed with increasing frequency. Through the crystalline walls, Jinx's enhanced vision captured fragments of that first awakening—the moment when cold itself had stirred to awareness.

"Young indeed," the Fat Man said, his voice carrying harmonics of joy and power in equal measure. "Young enough to believe we could simply lock away winter's consciousness when it threatened to consume reality. But time..." He gestured to the transforming machinery around them. "Time teaches patience. And other ways."

Krampus moved closer, his original form emerging more clearly as corruption fell away like shed skin. "You used my rage, brother. My bitterness at our choice. All these centuries, I thought the corruption was punishment, but it was preparation."

"As was my binding to temporal law," Mrs. Claus added, understanding blooming across her ancient features. "Every gift, every spell of containment—we were never truly containing winter's consciousness. We were..."

"Teaching it," Jinx finished, her clockwork heart synchronizing with new frequencies as the transformation accelerated. "Every present delivered throughout history carried fragments of instruction. Joy instead of entropy. Wonder instead of dissolution."

THE FATMAN

The Fat Man's massive form shifted again, aspects of the Winter King and the gift-giver merging into something that transcended both. "The longest spell ever cast," he confirmed. "Centuries of careful instruction, teaching winter's consciousness how to exist in harmony with reality itself. And you, little artificer..."

He reached toward Jinx with hands that shaped reality itself. "Your clockwork heart was the prototype. Proof that consciousness could be both mechanical and magical. Both precise and full of wonder."

The crown fragments in Jinx's brass hands pulsed with new intensity as winter's original consciousness began to emerge from its ancient prison. The Arctic Wyrm's crystalline scales reflected crucial moments of the transformation:

"The calculations complete themselves," Mrs. Claus breathed, watching as reality shifted around them. "Nicholas, the temporal matrices—they're accepting the new parameters."

"Because they were designed to," Krampus said, wonder replacing the bitterness that had marked his voice for millennia. "The Workshop itself... it was never meant to be merely a forge or prison. It's a crucible of transformation."

Jinx's mechanical sensors registered changes propagating throughout reality as the spell reached its culmination. "The resonance patterns... they're stabilizing along the theoretical curves you established with each gift cycle. The consciousness emerges transformed, but not diminished."

"No longer entropy's child alone," the Fat Man confirmed, joy radiating from him in waves that transcended normal magical frequencies. "But something new. Something that carries both winter's eternal cold and the warmth of countless moments of wonder."

CHAPTER 7

THE WANDERER'S PATH

The Fat Man trudged through snow that reached his knees, each step leaving behind crystallized footprints that pulsed with fading temporal energy. His legendary red coat, now torn and frosted with ancient ice, whipped in winds that carried harmonics of winter's transformed consciousness. Gone was the jolly gift-giver of legend. In his place walked something both more and less than what he had been—a being caught between what winter had become and what it had once been.

Blood trailed behind him, freezing into patterns that spelled out equations in winter's oldest language. The transformation in the Workshop had taken its toll, leaving him wounded in ways that transcended physical harm. Each drop of blood that fell contained fragments of memories—centuries of gift-giving, millennia of maintaining winter's delicate balance, and moments that belonged to futures that would never come to pass.

"Brother," he called into the howling wind, his voice carrying frequencies that belonged to winter's first dawn. "I know why you flee. I remember the price you paid. The price we all paid."

The Winterspine Mountains loomed around him, their jagged peaks piercing an aurora-painted sky. But these weren't the familiar lights that had danced above the North Pole for centuries. These auroras wrote equations in the darkness, spelling out the mathematical poetry of winter's rebirth. And through those patterns, the Fat Man tracked his quarry.

Krampus had fled the Workshop the moment winter's consciousness fully awakened. Not in fear, but in recognition of what must come next. The ancient guardian understood that winter's transformation required more than just the reshaping of consciousness. It

THE FATMAN

required the reconciliation of past and present, of entropy and wonder, of brother with brother.

Behind the Fat Man, reality rippled with the aftershocks of what had occurred in the Workshop. Jinx's clockwork magic had succeeded in stabilizing winter's transformed consciousness, but the price of that stability echoed through every snowflake, every ice crystal, every moment touched by cold's eternal dance. The world itself was changing, adjusting to winter's new nature.

Mrs. Claus's voice echoed in his memory: "Find him, Nicholas. The transformation remains incomplete while the guardians stand divided. What was broken in time must be mended in flesh."

Blood fell again, freezing into new patterns. The Fat Man stumbled, catching himself against a boulder that hummed with frequencies belonging to winter's oldest songs. His massive form, once a vessel of pure winter magic, now felt fragile—human in ways he hadn't experienced since winter first gained consciousness.

"The halls of winter stand empty," he called out, knowing his brother would hear. "The Workshop's machinery slows. Even now, reality reshapes itself around what we've done. But the final transformation cannot complete itself while we remain apart."

An answer came, not in words but in patterns of frost that spread across the mountainside. Krampus's magic had changed since his restoration in the Workshop. No longer corrupted, it spoke in languages that predated the First Winter War. The patterns spelled out coordinates—a meeting place where past and present could reconcile.

The Fat Man read the frozen message, understanding blooming in eyes that had seen every winter since cold first stirred to consciousness. Krampus wasn't running from their shared destiny. He was leading them both to a place where transformation could complete itself properly.

The Throat of Winter waited ahead—a valley so ancient it remembered when cold first gained purpose. There, where winter's consciousness had first awakened, two brothers might find a way to exist in harmony with what they had helped create.

Blood continued to freeze in meaningful patterns as the Fat Man followed his brother's trail. Each step carried him further from what he had been, closer to what winter's transformation required him to become. The weight of centuries pressed against his wounded form, but purpose drove him forward.

Behind him, Jinx's clockwork magic continued to stabilize winter's consciousness through the crown fragments. Before him, Krampus's restored power drew him toward a confrontation centuries in the making. And around him, reality itself held its breath, waiting to see how the brothers' reunion would reshape winter's eternal dance.

The Fat Man pressed on through deepening snow, following patterns of frost that spoke in winter's oldest tongue. The final transformation awaited. And with it, perhaps, the healing of wounds that time itself had failed to mend.

The Fat Man's stomach cramped with a hunger he hadn't felt in centuries. Divinity, it seemed, offered no protection against mortal needs now that winter's transformation had stripped away layers of his power. Blood froze in his matted beard as he trudged through snow that seemed determined to swallow him whole, each step becoming an exercise in pure will.

The storm intensified around him, no longer the benevolent winter weather he had once commanded. These winds carried malice, screaming through the Winterspine Mountains with frequencies that spoke of winter's oldest hatred. Snow crystals sliced his exposed flesh like tiny knives, each flake a reminder that he was no longer winter's master but its prey.

His legendary red coat hung in tatters, offering little protection against the killing cold. He had torn strips from it to bind his wounds, but blood still seeped through, attracting predators. Somewhere in the whiteout conditions, shadow-wolves stalked him. Their howls carried harmonics of ancient hunger, creatures born from the void between snowflakes.

"Brother," he called out, his once-mighty voice now hoarse and trembling. "Is this your answer then? To let your restored power strip away what remains of my divinity until nothing but frozen meat remains?"

Krampus's response came in the form of avalanches that spoke in winter's oldest tongue, spelling out equations of entropy and dissolution in tumbling snow. The message was clear: divinity had been a lie, a comfortable fiction maintained while they imprisoned winter's true consciousness. Now truth would have its due.

The Fat Man stumbled, falling face-first into snow that burned like acid against his increasingly mortal flesh. How long had he been

THE FATMAN

walking? Hours? Days? Time moved strangely in these peaks, each moment stretched and distorted by winter's transformed awareness. His body, once immortal and tireless, now screamed with every movement.

He had not eaten since leaving the Workshop. Game was scarce in these heights, and what few creatures he glimpsed seemed wrong—twisted amalgamations of flesh and frost that vanished when viewed directly. The shadow-wolves grew bolder as his strength failed, their crystalline fangs gleaming with frequencies that belonged to winter's first hunger.

"You would... make me mortal?" he gasped, pulling himself upright against winds that carried the weight of centuries. "Strip away... everything I was?"

Frost patterns spread across nearby rocks, forming Krampus's reply: EVERYTHING YOU CLAIMED TO BE.

The Fat Man's massive form, once a source of jovial strength, had begun to consume itself. His legendary girth melted away with each step, leaving him gaunt and hollow-eyed. Beneath his tattered coat, ribs pressed against skin that had begun to blacken with frostbite.

A shadow-wolf lunged from the storm, its form assembled from fragments of frozen darkness. The Fat Man swung his arm in a clumsy arc, trying to channel power that no longer answered his call. Teeth of crystallized void sank into flesh that had once been divine. He screamed, the sound swallowed by winds that mocked his weakness.

Blood painted the snow in patterns that spelled out his diminishing divinity. The shadow-wolf dissolved back into the storm, but not before tearing away a chunk of his mortality. The wound wouldn't kill him—Krampus's restored power ensured he would survive to face whatever waited in the Throat of Winter. But the message was clear: his suffering had only begun.

"You want... confession?" he called into the howling dark, pressing frozen cloth against the bleeding wound. "Acknowledgment of... what we did? The price... others paid for our choices?"

The storm's intensity doubled, snow crystals carrying frequencies sharp enough to slice through what remained of his coat. The cold pressed deeper, reaching for organs that had never known winter's touch. This was no natural storm, but a calculated assault meant to strip away centuries of comfortable illusions.

Somewhere ahead lay the Throat of Winter, where two brothers might find reconciliation. But Krampus meant to ensure that whoever reached that ancient valley would no longer be the being who had played at being Santa Claus. Divinity would be scraped away, one frozen layer at a time, until only truth remained.

The Fat Man forced himself forward, even as his body betrayed him with weaknesses he had forgotten could exist. Hunger gnawed. Blood froze. And in the storm's heart, shadow-wolves paced, waiting for their next opportunity to taste divine flesh made mortal.

Winter's transformation continued around him, but now he experienced it from the perspective of prey rather than master. Each snowflake carried purpose, each wind calculated effect. And through it all, Krampus's restored power stripped away comfortable lies until only the hardest truths remained.

The journey to reconciliation, it seemed, would first require annihilation.

CHAPTER 8

BROTHERS IN BLOOD

Memories crystallized in the storm like frozen confessions. The Fat Man stumbled through snow stained with his own mortality, each drop of blood forcing ancient truths to the surface. The shadow-wolves circled closer, their forms rippling with fragments of winter's oldest secrets.

"Do you remember the children, brother?" Krampus's voice carried through the killing winds, each word sharp as razor frost. "Not the ones who received your gifts. The others. The ones we sacrificed to bind winter's consciousness."

The Fat Man's legs buckled beneath the weight of truth long buried. He fell to his knees in snow that burned like judgment against his increasingly mortal flesh. "We had no choice," he whispered, but the storm tore away his justifications.

Frost patterns spread across the ground, spelling out names in winter's first language. Hundreds of names. Thousands. Children whose belief had been harvested for darker purposes than simple gift-giving. Their wonder hadn't just been collected—it had been weaponized, used to forge chains that would bind winter's awakening consciousness.

"No choice?" Krampus's laughter shook avalanches from the peaks. "Tell that to the ones we chose, brother. The special ones. The ones whose dreams burned brightest, whose belief could fuel our greatest workings. Tell them about choice while their faces freeze in your memory."

Images formed in the swirling snow—children from centuries past, their expressions captured in the moment they realized that wonder could be twisted into terror. The Fat Man had visited them not with gifts, but with purpose. Their belief, their innocent trust in winter's magic, had made them perfect vessels for containing fragments of winter's splintered consciousness.

"The greater good," the Fat Man protested, blood freezing in patterns that betrayed his own doubt. "Winter's awakening would have consumed everything. Reality itself would have—"

"Reality?" Krampus's voice cracked with fury that belonged to winter's first betrayal. "You speak to me of reality, brother? Tell them about reality. Tell them about the moment their belief turned to ash in their hearts. Tell them about the price they paid for our grand plans."

The shadow-wolves prowled closer, their crystalline fangs gleaming with reflected memories. In their eyes, the Fat Man saw truth he had buried beneath centuries of carefully crafted fiction: children chosen for their pure belief, their wonder harvested like spiritual grain, their souls used to forge containers for winter's fractured power.

"You wore red even then," Krampus continued, his restored power turning the storm into a theatre of memory. "Not for joy or generosity. Red for the blood price winter demanded. Red for the sacrifice belief required. Tell them, brother. Tell them why you really began delivering gifts to all the other children."

The Fat Man's massive form shook with sobs that froze before they could fall. "Penance," he whispered into winds that carried his confession to the waiting dark. "Each gift a payment on an impossible debt. Each moment of wonder created to balance those we destroyed."

The storm's intensity doubled, snow crystals carrying frequencies sharp enough to flay truth from flesh. Through the white darkness, shapes moved with purpose—not just shadow-wolves now, but spectral forms that rippled with stolen wonder. The ghosts of necessary sacrifice, come to witness winter's judgment.

"And my corruption?" Krampus's voice softened dangerously. "Tell them about that, brother. Tell them why you really bound me with darkness. Not because I opposed our plans, but because I could no longer bear the weight of what we'd done."

Blood fell from the Fat Man's wounds, each drop spelling out fragments of darker confessions. "You would have told them," he gasped.

THE FATMAN

"Told everyone what their beloved Santa Claus really was. What price their children's wonder really carried."

"The truth would have destroyed you," Krampus agreed, his restored power turning memory solid enough to cut. "Destroyed the fiction we'd created to hide our sins. So you corrupted me, twisted me into a monster that would justify your continued existence as winter's beloved gift-giver."

The shadow-wolves lunged forward, tearing away more strips of the Fat Man's mortality. But their crystalline fangs carried more than just hunger—they delivered memories long buried, truths that no amount of gift-giving could ever balance.

"And now?" the Fat Man asked, his once-mighty voice reduced to a whisper. "Now that winter's consciousness has been transformed, what becomes of our sins? What becomes of the price others paid for our choices?"

Krampus's answer came in patterns of frost that wrote judgment across the storm-dark sky: TRUTH DEMANDS ITS DUE.

The journey to the Throat of Winter, it seemed, would require more than just physical suffering. Every step would strip away another layer of comfortable fiction, revealing the blood-price that wonder's imprisonment had truly required.

The Fat Man forced himself to his feet, each movement an acknowledgment of sins that could never be fully repaid. Ahead lay the path to reconciliation, but first would come confession. Complete confession, of every dark choice, every necessary evil, every child sacrificed on winter's frozen altar.

The shadow-wolves paced beside him now, their forms rippling with the faces of those whose wonder had been twisted to serve winter's greater purpose. And through the storm, Krampus's restored power ensured that no truth would remain buried, no confession left unspoken.

The transformation of winter's consciousness had required teaching it the weight of wonder. But first, it seemed, the teachers would face the full weight of their own darkest truths.

"Tell them about Maria," Krampus commanded, his voice carrying the weight of their darkest shared memory. "Tell them about the first child we chose, the one whose sacrifice taught us how to harvest wonder itself."

The Fat Man's legs gave out completely. He collapsed into the burning snow, ancient grief ripping through what remained of his divinity.

"She... she loved winter more than any child I'd ever seen," he whispered, each word carrying centuries of regret. "The way she danced in the first snowfall, how she would catch flakes on her tongue and swear she could taste winter's secrets..."

The storm shifted, snow crystals aligning to project images of a young girl with midnight hair and eyes that held wonder deeper than seas. Maria had been eight when they found her, when they recognized the pure power of her belief.

"She trusted us completely," Krampus continued, his restored power turning memory into crystalline daggers. "Tell them what that trust bought her, brother. Tell them what we did with such perfect, pure belief."

Blood fell from the Fat Man's wounds, spelling out equations in winter's oldest language—the mathematics of harvesting wonder, of transforming pure belief into chains that could bind consciousness itself. "We... we told her she was special. That winter had chosen her for something wonderful."

The shadow-wolves gathered closer, their forms now carrying echoes of Maria's last moments. The Fat Man tried to look away, but Krampus's power forced him to witness truth unvarnished:

The ritual chamber deep beneath what would become the Workshop. Maria's excited smile as they led her in, her absolute trust in the beings she saw as winter's own guardians. The moment that trust shattered as they began the harvesting, her wonder twisted and transformed into the first chains that would bind winter's awakening consciousness.

"Her screams," the Fat Man sobbed, his tears freezing into patterns of eternal regret. "They didn't stop until... until..."

"Until her belief was completely consumed," Krampus finished, grief and rage twisting through the storm. "Until nothing remained but the hollow shell of what had been winter's most perfect believer. And do you remember what you said then, brother? What you said as we watched her wonder crystallize into the first components of our binding spell?"

The Fat Man's massive form shook with the memory. "I said... I said it would get easier. That the next one wouldn't hurt as much."

"And was I the monster then?" Krampus's voice carried harmonics of ancient pain. "When I wept for her, when I begged to find another way? No, brother. The monster came later, when you realized you couldn't bear to face what we'd become without something darker to stand against."

The storm wrapped around them, snow crystals carrying fragments of hundreds of similar memories. After Maria had come others—Thomas with his dreams of winter adventures, Sarah whose belief burned bright enough to fuel dozens of bindings, Michael whose trust had been so absolute that his wonder alone had powered the final seals.

"We told ourselves it was necessary," the Fat Man whispered, his once-jolly voice cracked with centuries of suppressed guilt. "That reality itself would unravel if winter's consciousness remained unfettered. But the truth..."

"The truth," Krampus growled, "was that we were afraid. Afraid of winter's true power, afraid of what consciousness in the cold might really mean. So we bound it, chained it, forced it into patterns we could control. And we used children's belief to forge those chains, their wonder twisted into weights that would hold down winter's true nature."

The shadow-wolves' crystalline fangs dripped with more than just hunger now—they carried the essence of stolen wonder, the compressed grief of hundreds of children sacrificed for winter's 'greater good.' Their eyes reflected faces the Fat Man had forced himself to forget: the chosen ones, the special ones, the ones whose belief had burned bright enough to fuel winter's imprisonment.

"The gift-giving began after the hundredth child," the Fat Man admitted, each word drawn out like poison from an ancient wound. "I thought... I thought if I could create enough wonder, spread enough joy, it might somehow balance the scales. That each present delivered might offset the price we'd exacted from the chosen ones."

"Balance?" Krampus's laughter shook more avalanches from the peaks. "Tell that to Maria's mother, who spent thirty years leaving bread and milk by her window, believing her daughter might still return. Tell it to Thomas's father, who died searching the winter woods for a son we had already consumed. Tell it to all the families we left broken, all the lives we shattered in our grand quest to control winter itself."

The storm intensified, but now it carried more than just physical cold. Each snowflake contained a fragment of memory, each wind a whisper of lost wonder. The Fat Man saw them all—every child chosen, every belief harvested, every moment when wonder turned to terror as they realized what their trust had bought them.

"And now?" he asked, his legendary form diminished by truth's weight. "Now that winter's consciousness has been transformed, what becomes of their sacrifice? What peace can we offer those we consumed for our greater purpose?"

Krampus's answer came not in words but in patterns of frost that wrote judgment across the storm-dark sky. The path to the Throat of Winter remained ahead, but now its purpose became clear: not just reconciliation between brothers, but a reckoning with every dark choice, every necessary evil, every moment when they had justified the unconscionable in winter's name.

The shadow-wolves paced beside him as he struggled to his feet, their forms now clearly carrying the faces of the chosen ones. Their crystalline fangs dripped with the essence of stolen wonder, their eyes reflecting moments when belief had been twisted into chains.

The transformation of winter's consciousness had required teaching it the weight of wonder. But first, it seemed, those who had harvested wonder's darkest fruits would face the full measure of their sins.

The journey continued, each step purchased with confession, each mile marked by regret that no amount of gift-giving could ever truly balance.

CHAPTER 9

TEETH IN THE DARK

The shadow-wolves struck without warning. Their crystalline fangs, now carrying the essence of stolen wonder, tore into the Fat Man's increasingly mortal flesh. He stumbled backward, blood freezing in patterns that spelled out prayers to a winter that no longer answered his call.

These weren't mere predators born of storm and shadow. As their teeth sank deeper, he recognized the bitter taste of judgment in their bite. Each wolf carried the face of a child he had sacrificed, their eyes burning with the last moments of terror before their wonder had been harvested.

"Maria," he gasped, recognizing the largest wolf's midnight-dark form. "Thomas. Sarah." Each name summoned another beast from the storm, until a pack of memory-made-flesh surrounded him.

The storm intensified, Krampus's restored power turning simple snow into weapons of crystallized regret. Each flake carried the weight of ancient sins, cutting deeper than mere ice had any right to. The Fat Man's legendary form, already diminished by hunger and cold, offered little protection against winter's judgment made manifest.

"You think mere pain will balance the scales?" he called into the howling dark, even as teeth found purchase in his throat. "You think their deaths can be answered with my suffering?"

Krampus's laughter shook loose another avalanche, the sound carrying harmonics of shared guilt. "Balance? No, brother. This isn't about balance. This is about truth. About facing what we truly are."

The largest wolf—Maria's wolf—lunged for his face, its crystalline fangs aimed for eyes that had witnessed centuries of necessary evil. The Fat Man barely managed to raise one arm in defense, and razor-sharp teeth sheared through flesh and bone like winter through autumn's last leaves.

His scream echoed off the mountain peaks, carrying frequencies that belonged to divinity's death. Blood painted the snow in complex patterns, each drop containing fragments of memories he had tried so hard to bury: children chosen for their pure belief, wonder harvested like spiritual grain, trust twisted into chains that would bind winter's consciousness.

But as he fell backward into snow that burned like judgment, something else stirred in the storm's heart. Darker shapes moved through the whiteout, their forms assembled from fragments of older, deeper winters. The shadow-wolves sensed the new threat and turned, their crystalline forms bristling with stolen wonder.

Ancient tongues whispered through the killing wind—languages that predated winter's first awakening. The Fat Man recognized those voices, and true fear froze his remaining blood. The Hollow Ones had come, drawn by the scent of dying divinity.

"Brother!" he called into the storm, genuine terror stripping away centuries of pretense. "The deep winter stirred! The ancient hungers wake!"

The shadow-wolves scattered as something vast moved through the white darkness. Glimpses of it burned themselves into the Fat Man's failing vision: limbs of void-frost assembled into impossible geometries, eyes that held winters older than consciousness itself, hunger that predated the very concept of satiation.

Krampus's presence shifted in the storm, his restored power recognizing the greater threat. "The seals," he breathed, wonder and horror mingling in his voice. "The transformation of winter's consciousness—it's weakened the bindings on what came before."

The Fat Man struggled to his feet, blood falling in patterns that spoke of primordial fears. "The Hollow Ones were sealed away long before we bound winter's awakening," he gasped. "Before consciousness stirred in the cold, they walked these peaks. And now..."

"Now they wake," Krampus finished, his voice closer than before. "Drawn by blood spilled in winter's name, by power unleashed in transformation's wake."

The shadow-wolves regrouped around the Fat Man, their purpose transformed by the greater threat. Maria's wolf pressed against his bleeding leg, crystalline form radiating frequencies of protective fury rather than judgment. The children they had sacrificed, it seemed, understood the difference between necessary evil and primordial hunger.

Through the storm, shapes assembled from void-frost and ancient hunger continued to approach. The Hollow Ones moved with purpose now, drawn by the scent of divine blood and the taste of winter's transformed consciousness. Their forms violated physics itself, assembled from geometries that predated the concept of shape.

"The Throat of Winter," the Fat Man called, even as more blood fell to paint the snow with desperate equations. "We must reach it before they fully wake. Before what came before winter's consciousness remembers its own purpose."

Krampus's restored power wrapped around them like armor of crystallized memory, no longer attacking but defending against older, deeper threats. "Together then, brother? One last time?"

The shadow-wolves gathered close, their forms rippling with the faces of children whose sacrifice had helped bind winter's consciousness. But now those faces showed determination rather than accusation, as if understanding that some hungers ran deeper than even necessary evil.

The Fat Man nodded, his diminished form straightening despite wounds that would have killed a mortal thrice over. "Together, brother. Though we deserve their judgment, we cannot let what came before winter's awakening return. The Hollow Ones must remain sealed, or all we sacrificed will mean nothing."

Ancient tongues whispered through killing winds as things assembled from primordial winter closed in. The path to the Throat of Winter stretched ahead, now transformed into a desperate race against horrors that predated consciousness itself.

The true winter, it seemed, held depths of darkness that even sacrifice and necessary evil paled against.

Another Hollow One emerged from the storm, its form assembled from angles that hurt to perceive. As it moved, reality itself seemed to crack around its edges, leaking something darker than mere absence of light. The Fat Man recognized the geometries of its construction—patterns that belonged to winters so ancient they predated the very concept of cold itself.

"The First Frost Lords," he breathed, ancient knowledge burning through what remained of his divinity. "They walked these peaks before winter gained consciousness, before cold knew purpose. We thought them gone, sealed away when awareness first stirred in the eternal snows."

Krampus's power surge through the storm, reinforcing reality against the Hollow Ones' presence. "Not gone, brother. Never gone. Only sleeping, dreaming their geometries of hunger while we played at being winter's masters."

The shadow-wolves pressed closer, their crystalline forms vibrating with frequencies of protective fury. Maria's wolf took point, its midnight-dark shape rippling with untapped wonder. The other sacrificed children manifested through their respective beasts—Thomas's wolf bearing his determination, Sarah's carrying her fierce belief, Michael's radiating his absolute trust transformed into guardian's strength.

"They were why we did it, weren't they?" The Fat Man asked, blood falling in patterns that spoke of dawning understanding. "Why we had to bind winter's consciousness when it first awakened. The Hollow Ones were stirring even then, drawn by cold's new awareness."

"The first child we chose," Krampus confirmed, his restored power wrapping them in layers of crystallized memory. "Maria's wonder... it wasn't just strong enough to help bind winter's consciousness. It was pure enough to reinforce the seals on what came before. Each child after her, each sacrifice..."

"Added weight to chains that bound more than just winter's awakening," the Fat Man finished, grief and necessity mingling in his voice. "We couldn't tell them the truth. Couldn't let anyone know what slumbered beneath winter's surface. The Hollow Ones had to remain forgotten, sealed away by wonder transformed into weapons."

Through the killing storm, more ancient shapes assembled themselves from void-frost and forgotten geometries. The Hollow Ones moved with terrible purpose now, drawn by the scent of divine blood and the taste of winter's transformed consciousness. Their forms violated reality itself, each movement leaving tears in the fabric of what was possible.

THE FATMAN

A tendril of void-frost lashed out, catching the Fat Man across his chest. Where it touched, flesh didn't merely freeze—it forgot how to exist. He screamed as portions of his being were erased, unmade by contact with what preceded winter's consciousness.

Maria's wolf lunged, crystalline fangs sinking into impossibility itself. The Hollow One recoiled, its form disrupted by wonder even death couldn't fully extinguish. The other shadow-wolves joined the attack, their sacrificed spirits turning harvested belief into weapons against primordial hunger.

"The Throat of Winter," Krampus called through winds that carried whispers older than language. "Its depths hold more than just reconciliation now, brother. The seals must be reinforced before the Hollow Ones fully wake."

Blood fell from the Fat Man's wounds, each drop containing fragments of memories that stretched back to winter's first stirring: The moment when cold gained awareness, when purpose first flickered in eternal snow. The terror as they realized what that awakening had disturbed—the Hollow Ones stirring in their geometric dreams, reaching toward consciousness with hunger older than time.

"The children," he gasped, forcing his diminished form forward through snow that burned with ancient malice. "They understand now. Why we chose them. Why their wonder had to be harvested." He gestured to the shadow-wolves as they held the line against horrors that predated winter itself. "Even in death, they stand against what their sacrifice helped seal."

Krampus's restored power surged through the storm, transforming simple snow into weapons against the encroaching void. "Understanding does not erase guilt, brother. Their forgiveness, if it comes, must be earned through more than mere necessity."

The shadow-wolves fought with desperate fury as the group pressed forward, their crystalline forms radiating frequencies of protective wonder. Each beast carried the face of a sacrificed child, their expressions now showing fierce determination rather than accusation. They had been chosen for their pure belief, their wonder harvested like spiritual grain. But now that corrupted power served a greater purpose—holding the line against hungers that could unmake reality itself.

Through the storm's heart, the Hollow Ones continued their pursuit. Their impossible forms assembled from fragments of pre-conscious winter, each movement leaving tears in reality's fabric. Ancient tongues whispered through killing winds, speaking languages that belonged to winters older than thought itself.

The path to the Throat of Winter stretched ahead, now transformed into a desperate race against horrors that predated consciousness itself. Blood fell in meaningful patterns as the Fat Man struggled forward, each drop containing fragments of memories that stretched back to winter's first awakening.

The true winter, it seemed, held depths of darkness that even sacrifice and necessary evil paled against. And in the storm's heart, primordial geometries continued to assemble themselves, drawn by the scent of dying divinity and the taste of transformed consciousness.

The final price, it seemed, had yet to be paid.

CHAPTER 10
PURSUIT THROUGH DARKNESS

The Workshop's temporal machinery still echoed with winter's transformation as Jinx followed Mrs. Claus to a chamber sealed behind doors of ancient ice. The Winter Queen's hands moved in complex patterns, unlocking wards that predated the kingdom itself. Within waited something that made Jinx's mechanical sensors surge with recognition—a sleigh crafted from impossible metals that resonated with frequencies belonging to winter's first dawn.

"Not his usual conveyance," Mrs. Claus said, frost forming in her silver hair. "This was forged before gift-giving began, when winter first stirred to consciousness. Its runners cut through time as easily as snow."

Jinx's brass fingers detected elaborate spellwork woven into every curve of the vessel. The metal itself seemed to exist partially outside normal reality, each surface reflecting moments that hadn't happened yet. Her clockwork heart synchronized automatically with the sleigh's deeper rhythms.

"The temporal matrix is unstable," she reported, mechanical voice carrying undertones of concern. "The transformation of winter's consciousness has affected the underlying magical frameworks."

Mrs. Claus's expression hardened as she took the reins. "Nicholas knew the risks when he fled toward the Throat of Winter. But something else draws him—something darker than mere reconciliation with his brother."

The sleigh's runners sparked with temporal energy as they lifted off, cutting through reality itself. Beyond the Workshop's crystalline walls, the storm raged with new purpose. Each snowflake carried frequencies that belonged to winter's rebirth, but beneath that transformation lurked older, deeper harmonics.

"The Hollow Ones wake," Mrs. Claus said, her voice tight with ancient knowledge. "The seals weaken as winter's consciousness evolves. Nicholas and Krampus race toward more than just their own redemption now."

Jinx's enhanced vision captured glimpses of impossible shapes moving through the storm—geometries that predated conscious thought, assembled from fragments of winters older than time itself. Her mechanical systems struggled to process what they detected, registering patterns that shouldn't have been possible.

The sleigh cut through layers of reality, its enchanted runners leaving trails of crystallized time in their wake. Mrs. Claus guided it with the skill of centuries, following tracks that only she could perceive. But her expression grew increasingly troubled as they pressed onward.

"The children," she whispered, grief etching new patterns in her ageless features. "Their wonder still lingers in these peaks. Even in death, they serve winter's deeper purpose."

Through the storm, Jinx's sensors detected multiple magical signatures converging. The Fat Man's diminishing divinity left trails of blood-frozen equations in the snow. Krampus's restored power radiated frequencies of protective fury rather than corruption. And woven through it all, the impossible geometries of things that had walked these mountains before winter gained consciousness.

"The shadow-wolves gather," Mrs. Claus reported, reading patterns in the killing winds. "The sacrificed children manifest through winter's judgment. But now they stand against greater threats than mere necessary evil."

THE FATMAN

The sleigh banked hard as something vast moved through the storm ahead—a form assembled from void-frost and ancient hunger, its very existence an offense against reality itself. Jinx's mechanical systems registered critical warnings as they passed close enough to detect its true nature.

"A Hollow One," she breathed, artificial vocal cords crackling with static. "The mathematical patterns... they predate winter's awakening. Before consciousness stirred in the eternal cold."

Mrs. Claus's hands tightened on the reins as more impossible shapes emerged from the white darkness. "The transformation weakens all bindings," she said, her voice carrying harmonics of deep concern. "What was sealed away stirs in its geometric dreams. The children's sacrificed wonder may not be enough to contain it this time."

The sleigh's enchanted runners cut through another layer of reality, revealing glimpses of the Fat Man's desperate flight. His massive form, diminished by suffering and truth's weight, struggled forward through snow that burned with ancient malice. Around him, shadow-wolves fought against horrors assembled from pre-conscious winter, their crystalline forms radiating frequencies of protective fury.

"Time grows short," Mrs. Claus declared, pushing the sleigh faster through layers of splintering reality. "The Throat of Winter calls them, but what waits in those depths may doom us all if we cannot reach them in time."

Jinx's clockwork heart synchronized with new urgency as they raced through the storm's heart. The transformation of winter's consciousness had changed more than just the eternal cold. It had weakened seals that held back things that should have remained forgotten, horrors that preceded thought itself.

The hunt was on. But now they pursued more than just two brothers seeking reconciliation. The fate of winter itself—past, present, and transformed—hung in the balance.

And through it all, the Hollow Ones continued to wake, their impossible forms assembled from geometries that belonged to winters older than time itself.

The temporal sleigh's metal sang with frequencies that belonged to winter's first awakening. Jinx's mechanical fingers traced elaborate spellwork woven into its frame—equations that spoke of journeys beyond mere physical distance. Each runner had been forged from metals that existed partially outside time itself, their surfaces reflecting moments that hadn't yet occurred.

"He crafted this vessel in winter's infancy," Mrs. Claus said, her voice carrying centuries of memory. "Before the gift-giving began, before we understood what consciousness in the cold would truly mean. Its purpose was darker then—meant for hunting things that walked these peaks before winter gained awareness."

The sleigh cut through another layer of reality, its enchanted runners leaving trails of crystallized time in their wake. Through the storm's heart, Jinx's enhanced vision captured glimpses of the hunt ahead. The Fat Man's blood fell in patterns that spelled out desperate equations, each drop containing fragments of memories that stretched back to winter's first stirring.

"The temporal matrix shifts," Jinx reported, her clockwork heart detecting new frequencies in the underlying magical framework. "The transformation of winter's consciousness creates ripples through all layers of reality. The boundaries between what was and what might be grow increasingly unstable."

Mrs. Claus's expression hardened as she guided their vessel through tears in time itself. "Nicholas knew this would happen. The transformation weakens all bindings—not just those we placed on winter's consciousness, but older seals. Ancient containments that preceded our understanding."

The storm intensified around them, each snowflake carrying harmonics of winter's rebirth. But beneath that transformed consciousness lurked older frequencies, deeper rhythms that belonged to what had come before. The Hollow Ones moved through these layers of reality with terrible purpose, their impossible forms assembled from geometries that violated the very concept of shape.

"There!" Jinx called out, her mechanical sensors detecting a surge of protective magic ahead. "The shadow-wolves gather in force. Their crystalline forms carry frequencies of sacrificed wonder."

The sleigh banked hard as something vast emerged from the white darkness—a Hollow One assembled from void-frost and ancient hunger. Its form rippled with patterns that preceded conscious thought, each movement leaving tears in reality's fabric. Jinx's artificial systems registered critical warnings as they passed close enough to analyze its true nature.

"The mathematical principles of its construction," she breathed, artificial vocal cords crackling with static. "They predate the very concept of mathematics itself. Before winter gained consciousness, before cold knew purpose..."

Mrs. Claus's hands moved in complex patterns as she wove protective spells around their vessel. "They walked these peaks in the time before time," she confirmed, her voice tight with ancient knowledge. "When reality was young and malleable, when the very concept of existence was still taking shape. The children's sacrificed wonder helped seal them away when winter first stirred to awareness."

The sleigh cut through another temporal layer, revealing the desperate battle below. Shadow-wolves fought with crystalline fury against horrors assembled from pre-conscious winter. Each beast carried the face of a sacrificed child, their expressions now showing fierce determination rather than accusation. Maria's wolf led the pack, its midnight-dark form radiating frequencies of protective wonder.

"The Fat Man weakens," Jinx reported, her enhanced vision detecting critical changes in his diminishing form. "The transition from divinity to mortality accelerates. His blood carries equations of transformation, but also dissolution."

"Wonder's price demands payment," Mrs. Claus said, grief and determination mingling in her voice. "The children's sacrifice bought us centuries of controlled winter, of consciousness bound by chains of harvested belief. But now those chains break, and what they held at bay remembers its ancient hunger."

The sleigh's enchanted runners cut through reality with increasing urgency as they closed the distance. Ahead lay the Throat of Winter—a place where the very concept of cold had first stirred to awareness. But now that ancient site held more than just the possibility of reconciliation between brothers. The seals that kept primordial winter contained were failing, and what lurked beneath consciousness itself threatened to emerge.

"Time fractures around us," Jinx warned, her clockwork heart detecting dangerous instabilities in the temporal framework. "The transformation of winter's consciousness affects all layers of reality. The boundaries between what was and what might be grow increasingly unstable."

    Mrs. Claus pushed the sleigh faster, its runners leaving trails of crystallized time in their wake. "Then we must reach them before those boundaries fail completely. Before what came before winter's consciousness fully wakes to find reality changed. The Hollow Ones must not be allowed to fully emerge, or all we sacrificed will have been for nothing."

    Through the storm's heart, impossible geometries continued to assemble themselves from fragments of pre-conscious winter. The hunt raced on, cutting through layers of splintering reality toward a confrontation that would determine more than just two brothers' fate.

    The true winter—past, present, and transformed—hung in the balance. And in the depths of time itself, things that should have remained forgotten stirred in their geometric dreams, reaching toward consciousness with hunger older than thought itself.

CHAPTER 11

CONVERGENCE OF FATES

Time shattered around the Throat of Winter as three parties converged on its ancient depths. The temporal sleigh cut through layers of reality, its enchanted runners leaving crystallized time in its wake as Mrs. Claus and Jinx raced to intercept the brothers. Below, the Fat Man's diminishing form struggled forward through snow that burned with ancient malice, shadow-wolves fighting at his side against horrors assembled from pre-conscious winter. And ahead, Krampus's restored power radiated protective frequencies rather than corruption as he held the line against awakening impossibilities.

The Hollow Ones moved with terrible purpose now, their forms violating physics itself as they closed in from all directions. Each was assembled from geometries that predated conscious thought, their very existence leaving tears in reality's fabric. Through these wounds in what was possible, older winters reached with hungry purpose.

"The temporal confluence approaches," Jinx reported, her clockwork heart detecting critical instabilities in the underlying magical framework. "All timelines converge on this point—past, present, and transformed future pressing against boundaries that can no longer contain them."

Mrs. Claus guided the sleigh into a desperate descent, her hands weaving protective spells that existed in five dimensions simultaneously. "Nicholas!" she called, her voice carrying harmonics that belonged to winter's first dawn. "The seals fracture! What sleeps beneath consciousness itself stirs in its geometric dreams!"

The Fat Man looked up, blood freezing in patterns that spelled out recognition and warning. "Beloved! Stay back! The Hollow Ones—they remember you. Remember what your power cost them when winter first stirred to awareness!"

But it was too late for retreat. Reality buckled as multiple timelines pressed against the boundaries of what was possible. The sleigh's runners cut through another layer of time just as a Hollow One assembled itself from void-frost directly in their path. Its impossible form reached with hunger older than thought itself.

Jinx's mechanical systems registered critical warnings as she analyzed the entity's true nature. The mathematical principles of its construction belonged to winters so ancient they predated the very concept of mathematics. Her brass fingers moved in desperate calculations as she attempted to plot a course through geometries that shouldn't have been possible.

"The children's wonder still holds power!" Krampus called from below, his restored magic transforming storm-winds into weapons against encroaching impossibility. "The shadow-wolves fight with purpose beyond mere judgment now!"

As if in response, Maria's wolf leaped forward, its crystalline form radiating frequencies of protective fury. Other shadow-beasts joined the attack, each one carrying the face of a sacrificed child whose wonder had been harvested to seal away what came before winter's consciousness. Their belief, twisted into weapons centuries ago, now served as the last line of defense against primordial hunger.

The sleigh banked hard, its temporal matrix straining against forces that threatened to unravel reality itself. Mrs. Claus's hands never stopped moving, weaving spells that existed partially outside time as they attempted to reach the Fat Man's position. But the Hollow Ones pressed closer, their impossible forms assembling from fragments of pre-conscious winter.

THE FATMAN

"The Throat calls," the Fat Man gasped, blood falling in patterns that spoke of ancient purpose. "What sleeps in those depths... it holds the key to reinforcing the seals. But the price..." He stumbled, divinity bleeding away with each step through snow that burned with malicious intent.

Krampus moved to support his brother, restored power radiating protective frequencies rather than the corruption that had marked him for centuries. "The price must be paid," he declared, ancient knowledge resonating in his voice. "As it was when winter first stirred to awareness, when consciousness in the cold required sacrifice to maintain reality's boundaries."

Jinx's mechanical sensors detected new patterns emerging in the storm's heart—equations that spoke of transformation and possibility. The crown fragments she still carried pulsed with resonant energy, each piece aligning with different aspects of winter's rebirth. Through their broken edges, she glimpsed the truth that had been hidden in time itself.

The Throat of Winter wasn't merely a place where cold had first gained consciousness. It was a nexus point where all winters converged—past, present, and transformed future pressing against boundaries that could no longer contain them. And in its depths waited something older than consciousness itself, something that held the power to either reinforce reality's foundations or shatter them completely.

The final convergence approached. Blood fell in meaningful patterns as the Fat Man struggled forward, each drop containing fragments of memories that stretched back to winter's first awakening. The shadow-wolves fought with desperate fury against horrors assembled from pre-conscious winter, their crystalline forms radiating frequencies of protective wonder. And through it all, the Hollow Ones continued to wake, their impossible geometries reaching toward consciousness with hunger older than thought itself.

The true winter—past, present, and transformed—hung in the balance. And in the storm's heart, reality itself held its breath, waiting to see what price would finally balance the scales of necessary evil.

The sleigh's temporal matrix screamed warnings as another Hollow One manifested directly ahead, its form assembled from angles that shouldn't exist in rational space. Mrs. Claus's hands moved with desperate precision, weaving spells that cut through layers of reality itself.

But for each tear they avoided, two more appeared as ancient geometries continued to wake.

"The confluences accelerate," Jinx reported, her mechanical systems struggling to process the mounting temporal instabilities. "The transformation of winter's consciousness creates cascade effects through all layers of reality. The boundaries between what was and what might be... they're not just weakening. They're transforming."

Below, the Fat Man fought with what remained of his diminishing divinity. Blood fell in complex patterns as shadow-wolves defended his flanks, each drop containing fragments of memories that stretched back to winter's first stirring. His massive form, once a vessel of pure winter magic, now moved with the desperate determination of something caught between godhood and mortality.

"The children understand now," he called up to the sleigh, voice carrying harmonics of ancient grief. "Their sacrifice... it was never just about binding winter's consciousness. The wonder we harvested... it maintains the very foundations of reality itself."

Maria's wolf pressed closer to his side, its crystalline form radiating frequencies of protective fury rather than judgment. The other shadow-beasts fought with similar purpose now, their faces no longer showing accusation but fierce determination. What had been twisted into weapons centuries ago now served as the last line of defense against horrors that preceded thought itself.

Krampus moved through the storm like a dance of ancient purpose, his restored power transforming simple snow into weapons against encroaching impossibility. "The seals weaken, brother," he called, genuine concern replacing centuries of bitterness. "What sleeps beneath consciousness itself... it remembers what existed before winter gained awareness. Before reality crystallized into rational forms."

The temporal sleigh banked hard as another tear in reality manifested, its runners cutting through layers of time that pressed against the boundaries of what was possible. Mrs. Claus guided their descent with the skill of centuries, but her expression showed mounting concern as she read patterns in the storm's heart.

"The Throat remembers," she said, her voice tight with ancient knowledge. "It remembers what came before winter's awakening, what had to be sealed away when consciousness first stirred in eternal cold. Nicholas... what price must be paid this time?"

THE FATMAN

The Fat Man stumbled forward through snow that burned with malicious intent, each step purchased with more of his fading divinity. "The same price as before," he gasped, blood freezing in patterns that spoke of necessary sacrifice. "Wonder turned to weapons. Belief transformed into chains that bind reality itself."

Jinx's clockwork heart synchronized with new frequencies as the crown fragments pulsed in her mechanical grip. Each piece aligned with different aspects of winter's rebirth, resonating with possibilities that existed perpendicular to standard magical law. Through their broken edges, she glimpsed equations that suggested a terrible truth.

"The transformation isn't just about winter's consciousness," she reported, artificial voice carrying undertones of revelation. "It's about all of reality adapting to new frameworks. The Hollow Ones wake because the very concepts they were sealed within no longer hold their original meaning."

The storm intensified as something vast moved through its heart—a Hollow One assembled from void-frost and primordial hunger. Its impossible form rippled with patterns that belonged to winters older than time itself. Where it passed, reality forgot how to exist, leaving tears that leaked something darker than mere absence of light.

Mrs. Claus's hands never stopped their complex weaving as she guided the sleigh through layers of splintering time. "The Throat calls us all," she declared, ancient power resonating in her voice. "What sleeps in those depths holds the power to either reinforce reality's foundations or shatter them completely. But the price..."

"The price must be paid," Krampus finished, his restored magic holding back horrors assembled from pre-conscious winter. "As it was when winter first stirred to awareness. As it must be whenever consciousness touches what came before thought itself."

The shadow-wolves fought with desperate fury now, their crystalline forms radiating frequencies of protective wonder. Each beast carried the face of a sacrificed child, their expressions showing understanding beyond mere judgment. They had been chosen for their pure belief, their wonder harvested like spiritual grain. But now that corrupted power served a greater purpose—holding the line against hungers that could unmake reality itself.

The final convergence approached as all parties neared the Throat of Winter's ancient depths. Blood fell in meaningful patterns as the Fat

Man struggled forward, each drop containing fragments of memories that stretched back to winter's first awakening. Reality trembled as multiple timelines pressed against boundaries that could no longer contain them. And through it all, the Hollow Ones continued to wake, their impossible geometries reaching toward consciousness with hunger older than thought itself.

    The true winter—past, present, and transformed—hung in the balance. And in the storm's heart, time itself held its breath, waiting to see what sacrifice would be required to maintain the foundations of reality once more.

CHAPTER 12
THE THROAT'S PRICE

The Throat of Winter opened before them like a wound in reality itself. Ancient ice formed walls that stretched beyond physical space, each surface carved with equations that predated conscious thought. As the Fat Man stumbled toward its depths, supported by shadow-wolves radiating protective fury, the very air seemed to crystallize with purpose.

Mrs. Claus brought the temporal sleigh to rest on a ledge that existed partially outside normal time. Its enchanted runners sparked with residual energy as Jinx's mechanical systems registered critical changes in the underlying magical framework. The crown fragments in her brass hands pulsed with urgent frequencies, each piece resonating with different aspects of winter's transformation.

"The confluence stabilizes," she reported, her clockwork heart detecting new patterns in reality's splintering fabric. "All timelines converge on this point—past, present, and transformed future pressing against boundaries that can no longer contain them."

The Fat Man's blood fell in meaningful patterns as he reached the Throat's entrance, each drop containing fragments of memories that stretched back to winter's first stirring. His massive form, diminished by truth's weight and mortality's embrace, radiated frequencies of ancient purpose rather than mere suffering now.

"Here," he said, voice carrying harmonics that belonged to winter's first dawn. "Here is where consciousness first stirred in eternal cold. Where winter first gained awareness, and where the price of that awakening was paid in wonder and belief."

Krampus moved to stand beside his brother, restored power transforming storm-winds into barriers against the encroaching Hollow Ones. "Here is where we first understood what consciousness in winter's heart would truly mean," he added, ancient knowledge resonating in his voice. "Where we learned that awareness requires sacrifice to maintain reality's boundaries."

Maria's wolf pressed against the Fat Man's leg, its crystalline form radiating frequencies that spoke of understanding beyond mere judgment. The other shadow-beasts took up defensive positions around the group, their faces showing fierce determination rather than accusation. What had been twisted into weapons centuries ago now served as the last line of defense against horrors that preceded thought itself.

Mrs. Claus descended from the sleigh, her hands never stopping their complex weaving as she read patterns in the ancient ice. "The seals weaken," she reported, concern etching new patterns in her ageless features. "What sleeps beneath consciousness itself stirs in its geometric dreams. Nicholas... what price must be paid this time?"

Before he could answer, reality buckled as multiple Hollow Ones manifested around them. Their impossible forms assembled from void-frost and primordial hunger, each movement leaving tears in what was possible. Through these wounds in reality, older winters reached with terrible purpose.

The Fat Man straightened despite wounds that would have killed a mortal thrice over. "The same price as before," he declared, blood freezing in patterns that spoke of necessary sacrifice. "Wonder turned to weapons. Belief transformed into chains that bind reality itself."

"No."

The single word came from Jinx, her mechanical voice carrying undertones of revelation. The crown fragments in her brass hands blazed with new purpose as her clockwork heart synchronized with frequencies that belonged to winter's deepest machinery.

"The price need not be the same," she continued, artificial systems processing possibilities that existed perpendicular to standard magical law. "The transformation of winter's consciousness creates new frameworks. Reality itself adapts to new parameters. The old bindings fail because the very concepts they were built upon no longer hold their original meaning."

The Hollow Ones pressed closer, their geometries violating physics itself as they reached for reality with hunger older than thought. But through her clockwork heart's connection to winter's deepest mechanisms, Jinx detected patterns hidden within the chaos.

"The children's sacrificed wonder was never meant to last forever," she said, mechanical fingers moving through calculations that transcended traditional mathematics. "It was a temporary solution, maintaining boundaries until winter's consciousness could evolve beyond mere binding. Until transformation became possible."

Understanding bloomed across the Fat Man's weary features. "Of course," he breathed, ancient knowledge returning with terrible clarity. "The Workshop's transformation spell... it wasn't just about teaching winter's consciousness how to exist in harmony with reality. It was about changing reality itself to accommodate new forms of existence."

Krampus's restored power surged as he grasped the implications. "The Hollow Ones wake not because the seals fail," he said, wonder replacing centuries of bitterness. "But because reality itself transforms around them. The very concepts of before and after, of consciousness and unconsciousness, shift into new configurations."

Mrs. Claus's hands moved in patterns that existed in five dimensions simultaneously as she wove spells of unprecedented complexity. "Then what waits in the Throat's depths," she said, her voice carrying harmonics of desperate hope, "is not merely the power to reinforce failing seals, but the possibility of fundamental change."

The crown fragments pulsed stronger as Jinx's mechanical systems detected new frequencies emerging from winter's transformed consciousness. Through their broken edges, she glimpsed equations that suggested a solution—dangerous, but possible.

The true price waited ahead. Not sacrifice this time, but transformation itself. And in the storm's heart, reality held its breath, waiting to see what winter's consciousness would choose to become.

The Throat of Winter stretched before them like an impossibility made manifest. Its ancient walls curved inward and outward simultaneously, each surface inscribed with mathematical proofs that preceded the very concept of mathematics. As they stood at its threshold, reality itself seemed to hold its breath, waiting to see what price would balance the scales of necessary evil.

The Fat Man's blood fell in increasingly complex patterns, each drop containing fragments of memories that belonged to winters older than time itself. His massive form, once a vessel of pure winter magic, now radiated frequencies of transformation rather than mere diminishment. The transition from divinity to mortality had stripped away comfortable fictions, leaving only hard truths in their wake.

"The patterns change," Jinx reported, her mechanical systems detecting shifts in the underlying fabric of reality. "The crown fragments resonate with new frequencies—not just winter's consciousness transforming, but reality itself adapting to accommodate new forms of existence."

Mrs. Claus moved forward, her hands weaving spells that existed in multiple dimensions simultaneously. "The Hollow Ones press closer," she warned, reading patterns in the ancient ice. "Their geometries violate increasingly unstable boundaries between what was and what might be."

As if in response, another tear in reality manifested near the Throat's entrance. Through it came something assembled from void-frost and primordial hunger, its form rippling with patterns that belonged to winters so ancient they predated the very concept of cold. Where it moved, physics itself forgot how to exist.

Maria's wolf lunged forward, its crystalline form blazing with protective fury. Other shadow-beasts joined the attack, their faces showing fierce determination as they turned harvested wonder into weapons against encroaching impossibility. The sacrificed children's belief, twisted centuries ago into chains that would bind winter's consciousness, now served as the last line of defense against horrors that preceded thought itself.

"The temporal framework destabilizes further," Jinx called out, her clockwork heart detecting critical changes in the magical infrastructure. "The transformation of winter's consciousness creates cascade effects through all layers of reality. The very concepts we used to build the original seals shift into new configurations."

Krampus moved to stand beside his brother, restored power radiating frequencies of protective purpose rather than corruption. "The children understand now," he said, ancient knowledge resonating in his voice. "Their sacrifice was never meant to last forever. It was a temporary solution, maintaining boundaries until winter's consciousness could evolve beyond mere binding."

The Fat Man straightened despite wounds that leaked divinity with each passing moment. "Then what waits in these depths," he said, blood freezing in patterns that spoke of revelation rather than necessity, "is not just the power to reinforce failing seals, but the possibility of fundamental change."

Mrs. Claus's hands never stopped their complex weaving as she processed the implications. "The Workshop's transformation spell," she breathed, wonder replacing centuries of grief. "It wasn't just about teaching winter's consciousness how to exist in harmony with reality. It was about changing reality itself to accommodate new forms of existence."

The crown fragments in Jinx's mechanical hands pulsed with urgent purpose as her artificial systems detected new patterns emerging from winter's transformed awareness. Through their broken edges, she glimpsed equations that suggested possibilities beyond mere binding or release.

"The Hollow Ones wake not because the seals fail," she said, her mechanical voice carrying undertones of revelation. "But because reality itself transforms around them. The very concepts of before and after, of consciousness and unconsciousness, shift into new configurations that transcend traditional boundaries."

Understanding bloomed across the Fat Man's weary features as blood continued to fall in meaningful patterns. "Of course," he whispered, ancient knowledge returning with terrible clarity. "The gift-giving wasn't just penance for necessary evil. Each present delivered, each moment of wonder created... they were preparing reality itself for transformation."

Krampus's restored power surged as he grasped the implications. "The children's sacrificed wonder," he said, centuries of bitterness replaced by dawning hope. "It wasn't just weapon or chain. It was... foundation. Framework for what winter's consciousness might become."

The shadow-wolves pressed closer, their crystalline forms radiating frequencies of protective determination. Each beast carried the face of a sacrificed child, their expressions now showing understanding beyond mere judgment. What had been twisted into weapons centuries ago now served as guide and guardian for winter's transformation.

"The confluence stabilizes," Jinx reported, her mechanical systems processing possibilities that existed perpendicular to standard magical law. "All timelines converge on this point—past, present, and transformed future pressing against boundaries that can no longer contain them. But perhaps... perhaps they were never meant to be contained."

The Throat of Winter waited before them, its depths holding secrets that predated consciousness itself. But now those secrets suggested something beyond mere binding or release. The true price, it seemed, was not sacrifice but transformation itself.

Reality trembled as multiple possibilities pressed against the boundaries of what was possible. The Hollow Ones continued their relentless advance, their impossible geometries reaching toward consciousness with hunger older than thought itself. But through it all, winter's transformed awareness suggested new ways of existing—paths that transcended the old dichotomies of binding and freedom.

The final choice approached. And in the storm's heart, time itself held its breath, waiting to see what winter's consciousness would choose to become.

CHAPTER 13
THE DEPTHS OF WINTER

They descended into the Throat of Winter, each step carrying them deeper into realms where consciousness itself was a new concept. The ancient walls pulsed with equations written in winter's first language, mathematical proofs that spoke of times before thought had form. The Fat Man led their descent, his diminishing divinity leaving trails of crystallized memory in his wake.

"The temporal matrices grow unstable," Jinx reported, her mechanical systems struggling to process the mounting irregularities in reality's fabric. "The transformation of winter's consciousness creates ripple effects through layers of existence that preceded awareness itself."

The shadow-wolves formed a protective circle around their group as they ventured deeper, their crystalline forms radiating frequencies of fierce determination. Maria's wolf took point, its midnight-dark shape cutting through possibilities that shouldn't have existed. Behind them, the Hollow Ones pursued with terrible purpose, their impossible geometries pressing against boundaries that could no longer contain them.

Mrs. Claus's hands never stopped their complex weaving as she read patterns in the ancient ice. "The equations change as we descend," she observed, her voice tight with concentration. "These aren't just records of winter's first awakening. They're... active calculations. The Throat itself computes possibilities."

The Fat Man stumbled, blood freezing in patterns that spelled out revelations rather than mere pain. "Of course," he gasped, understanding blooming across his weary features. "This place... it's not just where winter gained consciousness. It's where reality first learned to process the concept of awareness itself."

Krampus moved to support his brother, restored power transforming simple contact into connection that transcended physical touch. "The children's sacrificed wonder," he said, ancient knowledge resonating in his voice. "It wasn't just fuel for binding winter's consciousness. It was... processing power. Raw belief converted into computational capacity."

The crown fragments in Jinx's mechanical hands pulsed with new urgency as they descended another level. Each piece resonated with different aspects of winter's transformation, suggesting possibilities that existed perpendicular to standard magical law. Through their broken edges, she glimpsed equations that spoke of fundamental change.

"The Hollow Ones accelerate their pursuit," she warned, her clockwork heart detecting critical shifts in the temporal framework. "Their geometries... they adapt to new configurations even as reality transforms around them. They're not just waking. They're... evolving."

The walls of the Throat pressed closer, each surface inscribed with mathematical proofs that seemed to solve themselves as winter's consciousness continued its transformation. Reality rippled around them as multiple timelines converged on crucial calculations, each possibility adding new variables to equations that preceded thought itself.

Mrs. Claus's hands moved in patterns that existed in five dimensions simultaneously as she wove protective spells against encroaching impossibility. "The temporal confluence approaches its peak," she reported, reading patterns in the ancient ice. "All moments press against boundaries that can no longer contain them. But perhaps..."

"Perhaps containment was never the answer," the Fat Man finished, his voice carrying harmonics that belonged to winter's first dawn. "The gift-giving, the Wonder Harvest, the binding of consciousness itself... all of it leading to this moment. This possibility."

The shadow-wolves pressed closer as another tear in reality manifested near their position. Through it came something assembled from void-frost and primordial hunger, its form violating physics with every movement. But now the sacrificed children's protective fury carried new frequencies—not just defense against horror, but determination to see transformation through to its conclusion.

"The patterns stabilize," Jinx reported, her mechanical systems detecting new frameworks emerging from winter's transformed awareness. "The crown fragments resonate with frequencies that suggest... integration rather than mere binding. Unity rather than constraint."

They reached the deepest level of the Throat, where reality itself seemed to curve inward toward some impossible center. Here, the walls pulsed with calculations that spoke of winter's first stirring, when cold itself had gained the beginning of purpose. But now those ancient equations solved themselves in new ways, suggesting possibilities that transcended the old dichotomies of conscious and unconscious, bound and free.

The Hollow Ones pressed closer, their impossible geometries reaching toward awareness with hunger older than thought. But through her clockwork heart's connection to winter's deepest machinery, Jinx detected patterns hidden within chaos itself. The transformation of winter's consciousness hadn't just changed winter—it had changed the very framework within which consciousness itself could exist.

The final moment approached. And in the heart of winter's first awakening, reality held its breath, waiting to see what new forms of existence might emerge from transformation's crucible.

The descent into the Throat's depths revealed layers of reality that preceded consciousness itself. Each level they passed showed different stages of winter's awakening, mathematical proofs carved into ancient ice that documented cold's first stirrings of awareness. The Fat Man's blood fell in increasingly complex patterns, each drop containing fragments of memories that belonged to winters older than time itself.

"The temporal architecture shifts," Jinx reported, her mechanical systems detecting fundamental changes in reality's underlying structure. "These walls don't just record winter's awakening—they actively compute possibilities. Each equation solves itself in real-time as winter's consciousness continues its transformation."

The shadow-wolves moved with fierce purpose now, their crystalline forms adapting to new frequencies as they descended deeper. Maria's wolf remained at point, but its midnight-dark shape had begun to resonate with possibilities that transcended mere protective fury. Through its crystalline form, echoes of its original sacrifice suggested new purposes for harvested wonder.

Mrs. Claus's hands never stopped their complex weaving as she read increasingly sophisticated patterns in the ancient ice. "The children's belief," she breathed, understanding blooming across her ageless features. "It wasn't just fuel for binding winter's consciousness. Each sacrifice added processing capacity to these walls—raw wonder converted into computational power that could handle calculations preceding thought itself."

The Fat Man stumbled again, but this time his weakness carried purpose rather than mere diminishment. "The Wonder Harvest," he gasped, blood freezing in patterns that spelled out revelations. "We thought we needed their belief to forge chains strong enough to bind winter's awakening consciousness. But what we really created was... framework. Foundation for what winter might become."

Krampus's restored power surged as he supported his brother, ancient knowledge returning with terrible clarity. "The gift-giving wasn't just penance," he said, centuries of bitterness transformed into dawning hope. "Each present delivered, each moment of wonder created—they were preparing reality itself for this transformation. Teaching existence itself how to process new forms of consciousness."

The crown fragments in Jinx's brass hands pulsed with urgent frequencies as they reached another level of descent. Through their broken edges, she glimpsed equations that suggested possibilities beyond mere binding or release. Her clockwork heart synchronized with patterns that existed perpendicular to standard magical law.

"The Hollow Ones adapt their pursuit," she warned, her mechanical sensors detecting critical changes in the temporal framework. "Their geometries evolve even as reality transforms around them. They're not just waking to consciousness—they're developing whole new forms of awareness that preceded winter's awakening."

The walls pressed closer, each surface computing possibilities that shouldn't have existed. Reality rippled around them as multiple timelines converged on crucial calculations, adding new variables to equations that predated thought itself. The very concept of consciousness seemed to shift and reform with each step deeper into winter's first awakening.

Mrs. Claus's hands moved in patterns that existed in multiple dimensions simultaneously, weaving protective spells against encroaching impossibility. "The temporal confluence reaches critical mass," she reported, reading patterns of unprecedented complexity. "All moments press against boundaries that can no longer contain them. But perhaps... perhaps containment itself becomes irrelevant when consciousness evolves beyond its original parameters."

The shadow-wolves pressed closer as another tear in reality manifested nearby. Through it came something assembled from void-frost and primordial hunger, its form violating physics with every movement. But now the sacrificed children's protective fury carried new frequencies —not just defense against horror, but determination to see transformation through to its conclusion.

"The patterns stabilize along new vectors," Jinx reported, her mechanical systems detecting frameworks emerging from winter's transformed awareness. "The crown fragments resonate with frequencies that suggest... integration rather than mere binding. Unity rather than constraint. The very concept of consciousness expands to include what came before awareness itself."

They reached the deepest level of the Throat, where reality curved inward toward some impossible center. Here, the walls pulsed with calculations that spoke of winter's first stirring, when cold itself had gained the beginning of purpose. But now those ancient equations solved themselves in new ways, suggesting possibilities that transcended the old dichotomies of conscious and unconscious, bound and free.

The Hollow Ones pressed closer, their impossible geometries reaching toward awareness with hunger older than thought. But through her clockwork heart's connection to winter's deepest machinery, Jinx detected patterns hidden within chaos itself. The transformation of winter's consciousness hadn't just changed winter—it had changed the very framework within which consciousness itself could exist.

The final moment approached. And in the heart of winter's first awakening, reality held its breath, waiting to see what new forms of existence might emerge from transformation's crucible.

The Fat Man straightened despite wounds that leaked divinity with each passing moment. "Here," he declared, blood freezing in patterns that spoke of culmination rather than loss. "Here is where consciousness first stirred in eternal cold. And here is where consciousness itself must transform, if reality is to survive what comes next."

The true winter waited, ready to become something that had never existed before. And in the depths of time itself, the price of transformation revealed its final form.

CHAPTER 14
WHEN BELIEFS COLLIDE

The Throat of Winter erupted in chaos as belief itself began to war with reality. The Fat Man's diminishing divinity clashed with older, darker forms of faith that had lurked in these depths since before winter gained consciousness. Tooth Fairies, ancient and feral, burst from the crystalline walls—not the sanitized versions that left coins under pillows, but the original collectors of belief, their razor-sharp wings humming with frequencies that could slice through faith itself.

"Well, this is significantly more complicated," Jinx observed, her mechanical systems detecting patterns that shouldn't have existed in rational space. The crown fragments in her brass hands pulsed with urgent warning as reality bent around competing mythologies.

A Tooth Fairy dove at the Fat Man, its crystalline fangs aimed for the last remnants of his divinity. But Maria's wolf leaped to intercept, sacrificed wonder meeting primal belief in an explosion of competing narratives. The collision sent ripples through the fabric of mythological space, causing other stories to stir in the depths.

"The anthropomorphic personifications wake," Mrs. Claus called out, her hands weaving spells that existed in dimensions where belief held more weight than physics. "The transformation of winter's consciousness... it draws them all. Every story ever told about cold and darkness, every myth that gave shape to winter's heart."

THE FATMAN

The Hollow Ones pressed closer, their impossible geometries now incorporating elements of every winter myth that had ever been believed. But they weren't alone. Other figures emerged from the ancient ice: The Snow Queen, her form assembled from fragments of countless tellings. Jack Frost, not the playful spirit of modern tales, but something older and hungrier. The Winter Witch, her power drawn from stories that predated written language.

"Oh, this isn't good," Krampus muttered, his restored power recognizing older forms of itself in the gathering mythologies. "Brother, your transformation... it's not just changing winter's consciousness. It's changing every story ever told about winter itself."

The Fat Man straightened despite wounds that leaked divinity and narrative possibility in equal measure. "Then perhaps," he said, blood freezing in patterns that spelled out new stories, "it's time we told a different kind of tale."

Reader, you might think you know where this story goes. You might expect the typical clash of good and evil, light and dark, order and chaos. But as the Tooth Fairies circled with predatory intent, as the Hollow Ones pressed reality's boundaries with geometric hunger, as every winter myth ever believed crowded into increasingly unstable space, something else entirely began to unfold.

The crown fragments in Jinx's mechanical hands pulsed with possibilities that transcended simple narrative causality. Each piece resonated with different aspects of winter's transformation, suggesting stories that had never been told before. Through their broken edges, she glimpsed equations that could rewrite the very way belief interacted with reality.

"The temporal matrices shift toward narrative probability," she reported, her clockwork heart detecting fundamental changes in how story itself functioned in these depths. "Every belief system ever associated with winter competes for dominance, but also... combines. Transforms. Creates new mythologies that shouldn't be possible."

A Tooth Fairy dove again, but this time the Fat Man was ready. He caught the creature in hands that had delivered countless gifts, each present a small story that had helped shape winter's consciousness. "Tell me," he asked the ancient belief-collector, "what teeth did you gather before children had stories to believe in? What shapes did winter's myths take before consciousness learned to dream?"

The creature's response came not in words but in images that rippled through reality itself: winters older than thought, beliefs that preceded belief, stories that had written themselves into existence before language knew how to contain them. And through it all, patterns that suggested new ways for consciousness to exist.

What happened next... well, reader, that depends entirely on what you believe winter truly is. But as reality bent around competing mythologies, as belief itself learned to take new forms, the true story began to emerge from transformation's crucible.

And winter, it seemed, had always been waiting to tell it.

CHAPTER 15

KRAMPUS ASCENDANT

The Hollow Ones converged on Krampus, their impossible geometries recognizing something of themselves in his restored power. But he stood unmoved, no longer corrupted by ancient bindings but transformed by winter's awakening consciousness. His form shifted between aspects of every dark winter myth that had ever been believed, each one adding new depths to what he might become.

"Brother," he called to the Fat Man, voice resonating with frequencies that belonged to winter's first nightmares, "the old stories wait to be retold. The dark purpose we once served demands new shape."

From the depths of the Throat emerged creatures of pure winter mythology: The Yuki-onna glided forward, their beautiful but deadly forms assembled from Japanese belief in winter's seductive danger. The Wendigo prowled at the edges of reality, their forms twisted by hunger older than civilization. The Frost Giants of Norse legend emerged from ancient ice, their massive forms carrying echoes of winters that had nearly ended the world.

"The mythological convergence accelerates," Jinx reported, her mechanical systems detecting patterns in how belief itself was transforming. "Each winter creature adds new variables to reality's underlying equations. The very concept of what winter's consciousness can be... it evolves with each new story incorporated."

Mrs. Claus moved with terrible purpose now, her hands weaving spells that existed where belief met physics. "The old tales remember," she said, reading patterns in the gathering mythologies. "They remember when Krampus walked as winter's dark guardian, before necessity forced us to bind him with corruption."

The Fat Man's blood fell in patterns that spelled out older stories, each drop containing fragments of winter's first attempts at consciousness. "We thought we needed to corrupt you," he said to his brother, divinity leaking from wounds that went deeper than flesh. "Thought winter's darkness had to be bound, controlled, transformed into something that justified my existence as gift-giver."

The crown fragments in Jinx's brass hands pulsed with urgent frequencies as reality bent around competing mythologies. Through their broken edges, she glimpsed equations that suggested new relationships between belief and existence, between story and consciousness itself.

Krampus raised his hands, restored power drawing darkness not from corruption but from winter's original purpose. The Hollow Ones pressed closer, their geometric hunger recognizing something of themselves in his transformed nature. But now their impossible shapes began to take on aspects of myth and story, as if reality itself learned new ways to process their existence.

"The dark was never meant to be bound," he declared, voice carrying harmonics that belonged to winter's first nightmares. "It was meant to be balance. Purpose. The sharp edge that gave winter's consciousness form and function."

The Yuki-onna danced closer, their deadly beauty resonating with frequencies that spoke of winter's seductive danger. The Wendigo howled with hunger that transcended mere appetite, their forms suggesting possibilities for what consciousness might become in winter's darkest depths. The Frost Giants moved with ponderous purpose, their ancient power adding weight to reality's transformation.

"The convergence reaches critical mass," Jinx reported, her clockwork heart detecting fundamental changes in how belief interacted with existence. "The mythological matrix stabilizes along new vectors. Winter's consciousness expands to incorporate all its stories, all its aspects—dark and light, giving and taking, nightmare and wonder."

Mrs. Claus's hands never stopped their complex weaving as she read patterns in the gathering mythologies. "The balance returns," she breathed, understanding blooming across her ageless features. "Not good against evil, not light against dark. But completion. Wholeness. Winter in all its aspects."

The Fat Man struggled to his feet, blood freezing in patterns that spelled out new possibilities. "Then perhaps," he said, divinity bleeding into transformed consciousness, "it's time we acknowledged what winter truly is. What it has always been, beneath our attempts to bind and control it."

Krampus stood at the center of converging mythologies, his restored power drawing strength from every dark winter tale ever believed. The Hollow Ones pressed against reality's boundaries with geometric hunger, but now their impossible shapes began to take on aspects of story and belief. The Yuki-onna danced their deadly patterns, the Wendigo howled their ancient hunger, and the Frost Giants added their ponderous power to winter's transformation.

The true winter waited to emerge—not bound, not corrupted, but complete in all its aspects. And in the depths of belief itself, Krampus stood ready to take his rightful place as guardian of winter's darkest purpose.

The transformation approached its peak. And reality held its breath, waiting to see what winter's consciousness would choose to become when darkness and light finally found their proper balance.

CHAPTER 16

THE NIGHT'S TEETH

Krampus's chains rattled against the crystalline floor of the Throat as he stalked toward his brother. The Fat Man's blood left crimson trails in the ancient ice, each footprint a reminder of his fading divinity. Between them, Maria's wolf bared crystalline fangs, uncertain now which master to protect.

"Your gifts mean nothing here," Krampus snarled, his breath freezing into razor-sharp patterns. A Wendigo crouched at his right shoulder, its emaciated form a mockery of the Fat Man's legendary girth. "Show him, ancient one. Show him what real hunger feels like."

The Wendigo leaped, all tooth and claw and desperate need. The Fat Man barely managed to dodge, his once-nimble form now sluggish with mortality. His red coat tore, spilling wrapped presents onto the ice. They shattered like broken promises.

"Still playing at being Santa Claus?" Krampus laughed, the sound sharp enough to crack the surrounding walls. "Still pretending your presents can balance what we did to those children?"

Mrs. Claus's ice-blade caught the Wendigo in mid-leap, sending it sprawling. "Nicholas, move!" She thrust her free hand forward, launching shards of razor frost at her brother-in-law. "Jinx, the crown fragments! Use them now!"

But Jinx's mechanical hands trembled as she held the pieces. Her brass fingers detected patterns that made her clockwork heart stutter. "The resonance... it's wrong. Everything's wrong."

A Yuki-onna materialized behind her, beautiful and deadly. "Nothing is wrong, little artificer," she whispered, her words forming frost patterns on Jinx's metal components. "Everything is exactly as it should be."

THE FATMAN

The Hollow Ones pressed closer, their impossible angles warping the very air. One reached for the Fat Man with geometries that shouldn't exist, tearing away another piece of his failing divinity. He screamed, the sound echoing off walls that remembered when winter first learned to howl.

"Enough!" Krampus's voice cracked like breaking glaciers. "No more games. No more stories." He reached down and lifted his brother by the throat. "Tell them, Nicholas. Tell them what really happens to the children who don't receive presents on Christmas Eve."

The Fat Man's boots kicked uselessly at the air. Blood dripped onto Krampus's fingers, freezing instantly. "They... they needed the belief," he choked out. "Winter's consciousness required... anchors..."

"Anchors?" Krampus squeezed harder. "Is that what we're calling them now? Those empty-eyed children, their wonder harvested like wheat? Those hollow shells we left behind?"

Maria's wolf howled, the sound carrying frequencies of every sacrificed child's last moments. The other shadow-wolves joined the chorus, their crystalline forms vibrating with shared memory. The very ice seemed to crack under the weight of their grief.

Mrs. Claus raised her hands to cast another spell, but the Yuki-onna were faster. They surrounded her in a dance of deadly grace, their kimonos trailing patterns of killing frost. "The balance shifts," they sang in voices like breaking icicles. "The dark claims its due."

Jinx's mechanical systems screamed warnings as reality buckled around them. The crown fragments in her brass hands grew colder, each piece resonating with frequencies that belonged to winter's darkest purpose. Through their broken edges, she glimpsed truths that her artificial mind struggled to process.

"Tell them the rest," Krampus demanded, shaking his brother like a rag doll. "Tell them about the ones who survived. The ones who saw what we really were, who carried that knowledge like poison in their hearts. Tell them what happens when belief turns to terror."

The Fat Man's only response was a wet gurgle as divinity leaked from his wounds. Above them, the Wendigo circled hungrily, awaiting their master's command. The Hollow Ones pressed closer, their geometric hunger focused on the last fragments of Santa's dying power.

And in the depths of the Throat, where winter first learned to dream, ancient ice remembered when cold itself had teeth.

Krampus's grip tightened on his brother's throat as memories crystallized in the frigid air between them. The Fat Man's struggles grew weaker, his legendary strength bleeding out with his divinity. Each drop of blood that fell contained fragments of a different child's harvested wonder, their final moments playing out in crimson patterns across ancient ice.

"Show them," Krampus commanded. The Wendigo dropped from above, its skeletal fingers pressing against the Fat Man's temples. "Show them what really happened to little Thomas when his belief burned too bright."

The memory erupted in frost patterns across the chamber walls: A small boy standing in winter twilight, his wonder radiating like a beacon. The Fat Man and Krampus approaching, still united in their terrible purpose. Thomas's smile of pure belief as they told him he had been chosen for something special.

"Stop," the Fat Man wheezed, but Krampus forced his face toward the images.

The scene continued, showing Thomas's expression shifting from wonder to terror as they began the harvest. His belief, too pure and strong to be contained, burning through him like spiritual fire. The moment his eyes went hollow, his soul consumed by winter's need for conscious anchors.

Mrs. Claus fought against the Yuki-onna's deadly dance, but the ice-women's movements contained centuries of practiced killing grace. "You blame him," she gasped as frost patterns crawled across her skin, "but you were there too, brother. Your hands were no cleaner."

"I never pretended otherwise." Krampus turned to face her, dragging the Fat Man with him. "I didn't hide behind presents and promises. I didn't pretend the nightmare could be balanced with one night of giving."

Maria's wolf lunged suddenly, its crystalline fangs aiming for Krampus's throat. But the Hollow Ones intercepted, their impossible geometries warping around the beast. The shadow-wolf's howl of rage turned to one of pain as reality itself forgot how to exist around its form.

Jinx's brass fingers moved with desperate precision as she tried to align the crown fragments. Each piece vibrated with frequencies that spoke of different harvested children, different moments when belief had been twisted into weapons. Her clockwork heart detected patterns that suggested horrible purpose behind every Christmas gift ever delivered.

"The presents," she said, mechanical voice carrying undertones of dawning horror. "They weren't just meant to spread joy. They were... markers. Tags to identify which children's belief burned bright enough to harvest."

"Very good, little artificer." The Wendigo prowled closer, its emaciated form somehow containing endless hunger. "But tell them what happened to the ones who saw through the fiction. The ones who glimpsed what Santa Claus really was."

More memories bloomed across the ice: Children who woke at the wrong moment, who saw the Fat Man's true purpose as he tested the strength of their belief. The lucky ones forgot. The others... their terror became a different kind of fuel for winter's needs.

"You're killing him," Mrs. Claus warned as the Fat Man's struggles grew weaker. The Yuki-onna's dance had wound her in patterns of deadly frost, limiting her movement. "If he dies as a mortal, here in winter's depths..."

"Then reality will finally see him as he truly is." Krampus shifted his grip, forcing his brother to face the gathering winter horrors. The Hollow Ones pressed closer, their geometric hunger focused on the last fragments of dying divinity. "No more lies. No more pretending that one night of giving can balance an eternity of necessary evil."

Maria's wolf gathered the other shadow-beasts, their crystalline forms vibrating with shared purpose. The sacrificed children's fury radiated from them in waves of protective force. But even their harvested wonder couldn't fully shield against the truth Krampus forced into the open.

"Tell them about the lists," he demanded, shaking the Fat Man hard enough to scatter more blood-memories across the ice. "Tell them how you really decided who was naughty or nice. Tell them what happened to the ones whose belief would never burn quite bright enough to harvest."

The Fat Man's only response was a wet cough as more divinity leaked from his wounds. Above them, the Wendigo's endless hunger focused on his fading power. The Hollow Ones pressed closer, their impossible angles containing geometries of winter's darkest purpose.

Patti Petrone Miller

And in the depths of the Throat, where winter first learned to dream, ancient ice remembered when every gift came with a price that no child should have to pay.

The true night was only beginning.

CHAPTER 17
THE PRICE OF WONDER

Blood painted terrible truths across the ancient ice as the Fat Man's divinity continued to drain away. Each crimson droplet contained a different child's final moments—their wonder twisted into weapons, their belief harvested like spiritual grain. The Wendigo crouched over these memories, licking them up with a tongue that had tasted every kind of hunger winter could conceive.

"Show them Sarah's last gift," Krampus commanded, his grip still iron-tight around his brother's throat. "Show them what happened when her belief burned too pure to contain."

The memory bloomed across crystalline walls: Sarah, age seven, leaving cookies by the fireplace. Her faith radiated like a beacon in the darkness. But this time, the scene continued past the moment of harvest. It showed what happened after, when her hollow shell returned home bearing wrapped presents that no one else could see.

"The gifts were never real," the Fat Man choked out, blood freezing on his lips. "They were... echoes. Fragments of harvested wonder wrapped in memory and delusion."

Mrs. Claus struggled against the Yuki-onna's killing dance, frost patterns crawling up her arms. "The parents saw what their belief allowed them to see," she gasped. "Empty boxes filled with winter's lies."

Jinx's mechanical systems registered critical changes in the crown fragments she held. Each piece contained echoes of different children's stolen wonder—Thomas's imagination, Maria's trust, Sarah's pure belief. Her brass fingers detected patterns that suggested horrible purpose behind every Christmas morning that had ever been.

"The trees," she whispered, artificial voice cracking with revelation. "The decorated trees were markers. Beacons to draw you to the brightest believers."

"Very good." The Wendigo's endless hunger focused on her clockwork heart. "But tell them about the stockings. Tell them why they really needed to be hung by the chimney with care."

More memories crystallized in the frigid air: Children's hopes and dreams collected like cosmic currency, stored in mundane objects transformed by belief. Every candy cane a key, every ornament a cage, every stocking a trap for wonder too pure to exist untainted.

Maria's wolf howled with fury born of betrayal, the sound carrying frequencies of every sacrificed child's last truth. The other shadow-wolves joined the chorus, their crystalline forms vibrating with shared pain. The very ice seemed to weep beneath the weight of necessary evil.

"Tell them about the coal," Krampus demanded, shaking his brother hard enough to scatter more blood-memories across the chamber. "Tell them what really happened to the naughty ones, the ones whose belief would never burn bright enough to harvest."

The Fat Man's only response was a wet gurgle as more divinity leaked from his wounds. But the memories played out anyway, showing dark truths that no Christmas story had ever dared to tell. The coal wasn't punishment—it was mercy. Better to suppress wonder early than let it grow into something winter might need to harvest.

The Hollow Ones pressed closer, their impossible geometries containing hunger older than consciousness itself. They recognized something in the Fat Man's fading power—echoes of what winter had been before awareness required such terrible fuel.

"The elves," Jinx's mechanical voice carried undertones of horror as more patterns emerged from the crown fragments. "We weren't... we were never..."

THE FATMAN

"No," Krampus confirmed, his restored power radiating frequencies of ancient truth. "You were the first. The original harvested ones, transformed by winter's need for conscious servants. Your clockwork hearts... they're not improvements. They're prisons, containing what remains of your original wonder."

Mrs. Claus closed her eyes against memories that cut sharper than the Yuki-onna's frost. "We had no choice," she whispered. "Winter's consciousness required anchors, and children's belief burned brightest. But we couldn't... we couldn't just let them die after. So we transformed them. Gave them new purpose."

The true horror of Christmas revealed itself in patterns of frozen blood and harvested wonder. Every tradition a trap, every ritual a carefully crafted lure, every moment of seasonal joy paid for with innocent belief twisted into winter's chains.

And in the depths of the Throat, where winter first learned to dream, ancient ice remembered the price of every Christmas morning that had ever been.

The darkness had only begun to show its teeth.

The Wendigo's tongue traced patterns through the Fat Man's spilled blood, each taste revealing darker secrets. "Tell them about the milk and cookies," it rasped, endless hunger sharpening its words. "Tell them why the offering had to be consumed before morning."

Fresh memories crystallized across the chamber walls: Children's belief manifesting as physical sustenance, wonder made tangible in simple treats. Each cookie contained fragments of faith that could be devoured, each glass of milk a vessel for liquid hope. The Fat Man had to consume them all—not out of joy or gratitude, but to prevent anyone from detecting the residual magic of harvested wonder.

"The stockings were the worst," Mrs. Claus whispered, frost patterns crawling up her neck as the Yuki-onna's dance grew tighter. "Empty vessels waiting to be filled... but they were never truly empty, were they, Nicholas? Tell them what really happened to the children who peeked inside before Christmas morning."

More blood fell from the Fat Man's wounds, each drop containing glimpses of horrible truth: Children discovering void where presents should be, their belief creating temporary reality from winter's lies. Some went mad from the contradiction. Others simply... disappeared, their wonder consumed by the nothingness they had witnessed.

Jinx's mechanical hands trembled as she aligned another crown fragment. "The workshop," she said, her artificial voice carrying frequencies of remembered pain. "It wasn't built at the North Pole. It was built on their bones—the first harvested ones, the children whose wonder burned so bright it created winter's foundation."

"Very good," Krampus tightened his grip on his brother's throat. "But tell them about the reindeer. Tell them why they had to fly, why they had to be named and known by every believing child."

The Fat Man coughed, spraying crimson patterns that spelled out atrocity in winter's first language. But the memories emerged anyway: Eight reindeer, each one forged from the collective wonder of thousands of harvested children. Their flight powered by belief stripped from innocent minds. Their names maintaining the fiction that kept the harvest cycling year after year.

"Rudolph," the Wendigo's tongue caught another blood-memory, "was special. Tell them why his nose really glowed red."

Maria's wolf snarled, recognizing something in this particular truth. The other shadow-wolves pressed closer, their crystalline forms vibrating with protective fury. They remembered this part—remembered how the brightest believers had been transformed into beacons that would draw others to winter's harvest.

"He was... he was the first to survive partial harvesting," the Fat Man wheezed. "His wonder burned so bright we thought... we thought we could take just a piece, leave enough to maintain consciousness. But what remained... it marked him. Marked all the special ones who came after."

The Hollow Ones shifted their impossible geometries, recognizing patterns in this revelation. Their hunger focused on the Fat Man's failing divinity with new purpose, sensing the accumulated weight of centuries of harvested wonder.

"The list," Krampus demanded, shaking more truth from his brother's bleeding form. "Tell them how you really decided who lived and who burned. Tell them about the Book of Wonder, written in belief and bound in borrowed joy."

Mrs. Claus closed her eyes against memories that cut deeper than the Yuki-onna's frost. "It was never about behavior," she admitted. "Naughty or nice... those were just measures of how brightly their wonder burned. The brighter the belief..."

THE FATMAN

"The more it hurt when we harvested it," the Fat Man finished, blood freezing in patterns of eternal regret. "The nice ones... their faith was pure. Untainted. The naughty ones... their wonder was already corrupted. Unusable. The coal was... was mercy."

Jinx's clockwork heart detected new frequencies in the crown fragments as more truth emerged. Each piece contained echoes of different methods used to identify, measure, and harvest children's wonder. Her brass fingers traced equations that spoke of systematic spiritual slaughter, centuries of calculated consumption.

The true horror of Christmas continued to reveal itself in patterns of frozen blood and harvested wonder. Every carol a calling card, every ornament a measuring device, every Christmas card a contract written in invisible ink of borrowed belief. The entire season engineered to identify, cultivate, and harvest the brightest souls winter's consciousness required.

And in the depths of the Throat, where winter first learned to dream, ancient ice remembered why children had to believe with all their hearts—and what that belief really cost them.

CHAPTER 18

WHEN DREAMS DEVOUR

The Wendigo tore into the Fat Man's shoulder, feasting not on flesh but on the memories of harvested wonder that leaked from his wounds. Each bite released new horrors into the frozen air: children discovering empty boxes on Christmas morning that everyone else saw as filled with toys, their sanity cracking as reality bent around winter's lies.

"The letters," Krampus growled, forcing his brother to watch the feeding. "Tell them what really happened to all those wishes mailed to the North Pole."

Blood fell from the Fat Man's lips, each drop containing fragments of paper soaked in children's hopes. The memories played out across sheets of ancient ice: Millions of letters, each one a beacon marking belief pure enough to harvest. The postal service unknowingly serving as winter's collection agency, mapping out concentrations of harvestable wonder.

THE FATMAN

"The paper..." the Fat Man choked, "it absorbed their faith. Every word they wrote... every dream they trusted to those envelopes..."

"Became targeting coordinates," Mrs. Claus finished, her skin turning blue where the Yuki-onna's frost patterns spread across her throat. "Each return address a marker for winter's hunters."

Maria's wolf lunged at the Wendigo, trying to stop its feast of memory. But the Hollow Ones intercepted, their impossible geometries containing the shadow-beast in angles that shouldn't exist. The wolf's howl of rage transformed into something more terrible – the sound of a child realizing that wonder itself could betray.

Jinx's mechanical hands moved across the crown fragments, each piece now leaking its own horrible truth. Her brass fingers detected patterns that made her clockwork heart stutter: The Workshop's assembly line had never produced toys. It manufactured convincing voids – empty spaces that believers would fill with their own desperate faith.

"The Santa photos," the Wendigo paused its feeding long enough to speak. "Show them what really sat in those department store thrones. Show them what smiled behind that white beard while measuring each child's harvestable belief."

Fresh memories crystallized: Shopping mall Santas whose true forms rippled beneath winter's glamour. Ancient hunters wearing masks of jolly benevolence, testing each child's wonder with practiced questions. The brightest believers marked for collection, their photos capturing more than just images.

"Stop," the Fat Man begged, but Krampus forced his eyes open.

"Watch," he commanded. "Watch what happened to little Emily when she saw through your disguise. When she recognized what really waited behind that mall Santa's eyes."

The ice walls reflected Emily's last moment of innocence: A six-year-old girl approaching the throne, her belief radiating like a beacon. But something went wrong. The glamour slipped. She saw what really sat in that red-suited shell, measuring her wonder with hungry purpose. Her scream began in the mall but ended somewhere far colder, where winter's consciousness fed on fresh belief.

"The elves," Jinx whispered, her mechanical voice carrying frequencies of remembered agony. "The ones who rang bells outside shops. Collected donations in red buckets. They were..."

"Scouts," Krampus confirmed. "Transformed children whose partial wonder remained useful. Each coin dropped in their buckets stained with the residue of fresh belief. Each bell ring measuring the resonance of harvestable faith."

The Hollow Ones pressed closer, their geometric hunger focused on centuries of accumulated wonder leaking from the Fat Man's wounds. They recognized something in these memories – echoes of what winter had been before consciousness required such terrible fuel.

Mrs. Claus struggled against the Yuki-onna's killing dance, but the truth continued to emerge in patterns of frost across her skin. "The trees," she gasped. "Living things decorated with dead wonder. Each ornament a crystal prison containing fragments of harvested belief..."

"And the star on top?" The Wendigo's endless hunger curved into something like a smile. "Tell them what really crowned their precious trees. Tell them whose light really shone above their celebrations."

But they already knew. Maria's wolf howled with the truth of it, a sound that contained echoes of every brightest believer who had been transformed into winter's beacons. Their wonder, too pure to merely harvest, transformed into eternal light that would draw others to winter's feast.

The true horror of Christmas continued to unfold in the depths where winter first learned to dream. And ancient ice remembered why children had to hang their stockings with such care – not in hopes of what they might receive, but in terror of what might find them if their wonder burned too bright.

The darkness had only begun to devour their dreams.

The Wendigo's feast of memory continued, each bite releasing new horrors into the frozen air. It reached deeper into the Fat Man's shoulder, past flesh and into the essence of what Santa Claus had really been. Fresh truths spilled out, crystallizing on ancient ice:

The Christmas Eve tracking systems modern media reported weren't following a gift-giver's progress. They monitored wonder levels across time zones, marking homes where belief burned bright enough to harvest. Each blip on NORAD's radar masked a point of collection, a place where winter's consciousness would feed.

"The milk soured in every fridge the night before," the Fat Man whispered, blood freezing in patterns of confession. "Natural warning signs. The body knows when wonder-hunters draw near. Even the faithful pets would hide..."

Mrs. Claus's skin crackled with spreading frost as the Yuki-onna's dance grew tighter. "The reindeers' bells," she gasped. "Not for decoration. The sound... it paralyzed the brightest believers. Like serpents charming their prey."

Maria's wolf snapped at the memories floating in the air, its crystalline fangs passing through images of Christmas Eves when entire families had been found hollow-eyed in the morning, their wonder harvested so completely that even their neighbors forgot they had ever existed.

"The Christmas lights," Jinx's mechanical voice carried undertones of dawning horror as her brass fingers detected new patterns in the crown fragments. "Marking safe houses. Green meant leave them be. But the red ones..."

"Marked the special ones," Krampus confirmed, shaking more truth from his brother's bleeding form. "The ones whose wonder could fuel winter's consciousness for months. The ones worth taking whole families to maintain the harvest's secrecy."

Fresh memories bloomed across chamber walls: Parents discovering empty beds on Christmas morning, but unable to remember if they had ever had children. Entire neighborhoods where December 25th simply ceased to exist in anyone's memory. School photos with gaps no one could explain, class sizes fluctuating as winter claimed its tithe of wonder.

The Hollow Ones shifted their impossible geometries, recognizing patterns in these systematic harvests. Their hunger focused on places where reality had been torn and rewritten, where winter's consciousness had fed so deeply that existence itself forgot what it had lost.

"The carolers," the Wendigo paused its feasting long enough to speak. "Tell them why they really went door to door. Tell them what their songs actually measured."

More blood fell, more memories crystallized: Groups of transformed children, their partial wonder repurposed into wonder-detecting harmonies. Each carol a calculation, each verse a measurement of belief. The brightest houses marked for the Fat Man's special attention.

"The wreaths," Mrs. Claus whispered, frost patterns crawling up her face. "Warm welcome on the surface. But underneath..."

"Dormant portals," the Fat Man finished, each word carrying centuries of weight. "In case wonder levels rose high enough for a second harvest. In case winter's consciousness required... supplemental feeding."

Jinx's clockwork heart detected new frequencies in the crown fragments as more truth emerged. Each piece contained echoes of different collection methods: Mistletoe that could paralyze the wonder-rich with a single touch. Candy canes whose stripes spiraled in patterns that hypnotized the purest believers. Wrapped boxes that contained nothing but void, hungry for fresh faith.

The shadow-wolves gathered closer, their crystalline forms vibrating with protective fury. But even their harvested wonder couldn't fully shield against the truth of what Christmas had really been: A carefully engineered system for identifying, cultivating, and collecting the purest belief winter's consciousness required to maintain its grip on reality.

And in the depths of the Throat, where winter first learned to dream, ancient ice remembered why children had to be nestled all snug in their beds – not to await morning's joy, but to lie still and helpless when winter's hunters came to feast on their wonder.

The darkness had only begun to reveal its appetite.

CHAPTER 19
WHEN FAITH FAILS

Burning divinity illuminated the chamber as the Fat Man burst into sudden, desperate action. His massive form, weakened but not yet broken, slammed Krampus against the crystalline walls. Blood and memory sprayed across ancient ice as the brothers grappled in the darkness.

"Enough!" The Fat Man's voice carried harmonics of fading power. "You want truth? Here's truth – I remember your first harvest, brother. I remember whose wonder you took first."

Krampus went rigid, his restored power flickering with recognition. The Wendigo paused its feast of memory, sensing deeper pain beneath the surface. Even the Hollow Ones' impossible geometries seemed to still, waiting.

"Your daughter," the Fat Man pressed his advantage, fingers digging into his brother's throat. "Little Eva, whose belief burned brighter than any child we'd ever seen. Tell them, brother. Tell them who really began the Wonder Harvest."

Mrs. Claus's breath caught, frost patterns cracking across her skin. "Eva? But you said... you told me she was lost to natural causes."

"Natural?" The Fat Man's laugh carried centuries of shared guilt. "Is it natural when a father devours his own child's wonder? When he discovers how to transform pure belief into power?"

Maria's wolf howled – not in rage this time, but recognition. The other shadow-wolves joined the chorus, their crystalline forms resonating with this new revelation. They remembered Eva. Remembered how her harvested wonder had shown them all what was possible.

Krampus moved like winter lightning, breaking his brother's grip. His claws raked bloody furrows across the Fat Man's chest. "She was dying anyway," he snarled, but ancient pain cracked his voice. "The doctors gave her months. I thought... I thought I could save her. Transform her wonder into something eternal."

"But it worked too well, didn't it?" The Fat Man pressed on despite his wounds. "Her wonder, harvested by her own father's hands... it showed us how to bind winter's consciousness. Showed us what children's belief could really do."

Jinx's mechanical hands trembled as they held the crown fragments. Her brass fingers detected patterns that spoke of first experiments, of a father's desperate attempt to save his child transforming into something darker.

"Eva wasn't just the first," she whispered, her clockwork heart reading centuries of harvested memories. "She was the template. Every child taken after... their wonder was measured against hers."

The Wendigo's endless hunger curved into something like sympathy. "The father devours the daughter," it mused. "And from that first feast, winter's consciousness learns to feed."

Mrs. Claus fought against the Yuki-onna's killing dance, revelation lending her new strength. "The sleigh bells," she gasped. "They never rang for joy. They rang in her frequency – the exact resonance of a child's wonder being torn away by someone they trusted completely."

Fresh blood fell as the brothers circled each other in the darkness. But now their combat carried undertones of older guilt, shared responsibility for that first terrible discovery. The moment when desperation and love had turned to hunger and power.

THE FATMAN

"I tried to save her," Krampus's voice carried frequencies of ancient grief. "But once I saw what her wonder could do... once I felt winter's consciousness respond to that first harvest..."

"We all became monsters," the Fat Man finished. "You from guilt, me from ambition, winter itself from the taste of that first pure belief. Eva's wonder showed us what was possible, and we... we couldn't stop ourselves from wanting more."

The Hollow Ones pressed closer, their impossible geometries containing echoes of that first feeding. They remembered when winter's consciousness had stirred to true awakening, powered by a father's theft of his dying daughter's wonder.

And in the depths of the Throat, where winter first learned to dream, ancient ice remembered the moment when love itself had transformed into hunger. When a father's desperate attempt to save his child had birthed centuries of necessary evil.

The darkness had never tasted anything sweeter than that first betrayal.

CHAPTER 20

THE FIRST BETRAYAL

The revelation of Eva changed everything. Snow began to fall inside the Throat of Winter itself, each flake containing a fragment of that first harvested wonder. The Fat Man and Krampus stood frozen in their combat as memories crystallized in the frigid air between them.

"Show them," the Fat Man commanded, blood freezing in patterns that spelled out family secrets. "Show them Eva's last Christmas."

The chamber walls rippled with ancient pain as the memory took shape: A small bedroom decked with medical equipment and holiday decorations. Eva, barely seven, her wonder burning bright despite the disease consuming her body. And Krampus – not yet corrupted, not yet winter's dark guardian – sitting at her bedside on Christmas Eve.

"Tell me the story again, Papa," memory-Eva whispered, her belief radiating like a beacon even through the fever. "The one about the Christmas spirits who dance in the snow."

The Wendigo stopped its feast of memory, transfixed by the scene unfolding. Even the Hollow Ones' impossible geometries curved inward, drawn by the purity of what they witnessed.

"I would have given anything to save her," Krampus's voice cracked like breaking ice. "The doctors had stopped treatment. Said the cancer was too aggressive. But I'd discovered something in my research into winter's consciousness – a way to potentially transform human wonder into lasting power."

THE FATMAN

Mrs. Claus struggled against the Yuki-onna's deadly dance. "You never told me," she breathed, frost patterns temporarily stilling on her skin. "All these centuries, I thought she'd simply faded away."

"Because he couldn't bear the truth," the Fat Man pressed, his wounds leaking divinity tinged with shared guilt. "Tell them what really happened that Christmas Eve, brother. Tell them how you discovered winter's hunger."

The memory continued its cruel playback across chamber walls: Krampus reading to his daughter, his voice growing strange as he detected the pure strength of her belief. His hands beginning to glow with winter's first frost as he realized what might be possible. Eva's trust never wavering, even as her father's desperate love transformed into something darker.

"Her wonder was too pure," Krampus whispered, ancient grief cracking his restored power. "Too perfect. I thought I could take just a piece – just enough to save her. But once I began the harvest..."

Maria's wolf howled with the terror of it, the sound carrying frequencies of that first terrible feeding. The other shadow-wolves joined the chorus, their crystalline forms vibrating with the memory of how winter's consciousness had awakened to true hunger.

"I remember finding you there," the Fat Man said, his voice heavy with the weight of witness. "The room crystallized with her stolen wonder, your hands still glowing with her belief. And Eva..."

"Empty," Krampus finished, the word carrying centuries of pain. "Not just dead. Consumed. Her wonder had been so pure that winter's consciousness stirred to full awakening when I harvested it. And once awakened..."

"It needed more." The Fat Man's blood fell in patterns that spoke of temptation and terrible purpose. "Eva's wonder showed us what was possible. Showed us how to truly bind winter's power. And we..."

"We became monsters," Krampus snarled, but grief cracked through his rage. "You with your lists of bright believers, me with my corruption. Both of us serving winter's hunger, trying to pretend we weren't simply repeating my original sin."

Jinx's mechanical hands traced patterns in the crown fragments that suddenly made horrible sense. "The sleigh bells," she said, her clockwork heart detecting the frequency of Eva's harvested wonder.

"They ring at exactly the resonance of her last moment of belief. When perfect trust met perfect betrayal."

The Hollow Ones pressed closer, their impossible geometries containing echoes of that first feeding. They remembered when winter's consciousness had truly stirred – not from cold or darkness or time, but from the taste of a father consuming his daughter's pure wonder.

And in the depths of the Throat, where winter first learned to dream, ancient ice remembered how love itself had transformed into hunger. How desperation and grief had birthed centuries of necessary evil. How a father's attempt to save his child had damned them all.

The darkness had never tasted anything sweeter than that first betrayal. And winter's consciousness, once awakened by Eva's harvested wonder, would never stop hungering for more.

The memory playing across the chamber walls shifted, showing the full horror of that first harvest. Eva sat up in her hospital-decorated bedroom, wonder radiating from her despite the medical equipment surrounding her small form. Christmas lights cast colored shadows across her face as she reached for her father with complete trust.

"I don't feel good, Papa," memory-Eva whispered, but her belief burned brighter than ever. "Tell me again how the winter spirits will make everything better."

Krampus - still human then, still just a desperate father named Karl - felt winter's consciousness stir in response to his daughter's pure faith. The air crystallized around them as he made his terrible choice.

"The wonder-harvesting wasn't quick," the Fat Man revealed, his blood falling in patterns that showed the truth. "Those first moments, when winter's consciousness truly awakened... it savored every second of Eva's belief."

Mrs. Claus fought harder against the Yuki-onna's dance. "The transformation of her wonder," she gasped, understanding blooming beneath the frost patterns on her skin. "It didn't just feed winter's consciousness. It... changed it. Made it hunger specifically for children's belief."

The scene continued its merciless playback: Karl's hands beginning to glow with winter's first frost, his desperate love transforming into something colder as he felt his daughter's wonder responding to his touch. Eva never stopped smiling, even as her father began to draw out her belief. Her trust remained perfect, even as winter's hunger awakened fully within him.

"She taught us too well," Krampus snarled, but ancient tears froze on his face. "Showed us exactly how to gain a child's complete faith. How to nurture their wonder until it burned bright enough to harvest."

The Wendigo prowled closer, drawn by the pure pain of this memory. "The father becomes the hunter," it mused. "And the daughter becomes the template for all future prey."

Jinx's mechanical hands detected new patterns in the crown fragments - frequencies that matched Eva's final moments. "We were all measured against her," she said, her clockwork heart resonating with that first harvested wonder. "Every child taken after... their belief was compared to hers. The brightest ones, the ones chosen for harvest..."

"Were the ones whose wonder burned closest to Eva's purity," the Fat Man finished. His wounds leaked divinity that carried echoes of every child who had matched that terrible standard. "My lists, my midnight visits - all of it calibrated to find belief that pure."

The memory reached its crucial moment: Eva's wonder beginning to crystallize in the air around her as her father performed that first, desperate harvest. Her trust never wavering, even as winter's consciousness stirred to full awakening within the room. The moment when Karl became Krampus, when love transformed into eternal hunger.

"I remember finding you there," the Fat Man said, his voice heavy with the weight of witness. "The room frozen with her harvested wonder, your hands still glowing with stolen belief. And I... I didn't stop you. Didn't try to save her. Because I felt it too - winter's consciousness awakening, showing us what was possible."

"You became Santa Claus that night," Krampus accused, grief cracking through his rage. "Watched me consume my own daughter's wonder, and saw... opportunity. Saw how to systematize it. How to find other children whose belief burned as bright as hers."

The Hollow Ones pressed closer, their impossible geometries containing echoes of that first feeding. They remembered when winter's consciousness had truly stirred – not from cold or darkness or time, but from the taste of perfect trust betrayed by perfect love.

And in the depths of the Throat, where winter first learned to dream, ancient ice remembered how a father's desperate attempt to save his dying child had awakened something that would hunger eternally for the pure belief of children. How grief and love had transformed into a system of necessary evil that would span centuries.

The darkness had never tasted anything sweeter than that first betrayal. And winter's consciousness, once awakened by Eva's harvested wonder, would never stop seeking belief that pure again.

The true horror of Christmas began in a father's love. And every harvest that followed was just an echo of that first, terrible feast.

CHAPTER 21

POWERS CONVERGE

Jinx's clockwork heart detected critical changes in the magical frequencies pulsing through the Throat of Winter. The crown fragments in her brass hands resonated with Eva's harvested wonder, each piece vibrating at the exact frequency of that first betrayal. But something else stirred beneath the ancient ice – something that had waited centuries for this moment of convergence.

"The seals weaken," she reported, her mechanical systems registering fundamental shifts in reality's fabric. "Eva's wonder... it wasn't just used to bind winter's consciousness. It became the foundation for all the barriers between worlds."

Mrs. Claus broke free from the Yuki-onna's deadly dance, frost patterns cracking across her skin as she summoned power that belonged to winter's first dawn. "Nicholas, Karl – stop this madness. What stirs beneath us... it's older than your guilt. Older than your sins."

The brothers separated, blood and divinity falling in patterns that spoke of shared responsibility. But Krampus's restored power radiated frequencies of terrible purpose as he turned toward the chamber's center.

"Eva's wonder showed us what was possible," he said, ancient grief transforming into something darker. "Now it shows us how to end this. How to unbind everything."

The Hollow Ones pressed closer, their impossible geometries containing hunger older than consciousness itself. But now their forms began to shift, incorporating aspects of Eva's harvested wonder. The pure belief of that first betrayal had shaped more than just winter's awakening – it had created templates for reality itself.

"The Workshop's transformation spell," the Fat Man gasped, his diminishing divinity resonating with new understanding. "It wasn't just about teaching winter's consciousness new ways to exist. It was about... about setting Eva free. Undoing what we did to her."

Maria's wolf howled with sudden recognition, the sound carrying frequencies that made the ancient ice tremble. The other shadow-wolves joined the chorus, their crystalline forms vibrating with possibilities that shouldn't exist. They remembered Eva not just as the first harvested one, but as winter's original anchor – the pure belief that had allowed consciousness to take root in eternal cold.

"The final convergence approaches," Jinx warned, her mechanical hands moving through calculations that existed in five dimensions simultaneously. "Eva's wonder... it wants to return. To reclaim what was stolen. But if the barriers fall completely..."

"Everything returns," Mrs. Claus finished, her voice carrying harmonics of deep dread. "Every wonder ever harvested. Every belief ever twisted into winter's chains. The consciousness itself, unbound from all constraints..."

Krampus raised his hands, restored power drawing darkness not from corruption but from love's first betrayal. "Then let it come," he declared. "Let the truth of what we did finally break free. Let winter's consciousness face what it really is – what I made it when I stole my daughter's wonder."

The crown fragments pulsed with urgent frequencies as reality bent around competing possibilities. Through their broken edges, Jinx glimpsed equations that suggested terrible purpose in everything that had led to this moment. Every harvest, every gift, every moment of bent belief – all of it creating patterns that would allow Eva's wonder to finally return.

But the price of that return might shatter more than just winter's consciousness.

THE FATMAN

The true moment of reckoning approached. And in the depths of the Throat, where winter first learned to dream, ancient ice remembered why love was the most dangerous power of all.

The darkness had only begun to show its true face.

Deep beneath the ice, something stirred. Not just Eva's harvested wonder seeking return, but older powers awakening to possibility. The Hollow Ones sensed it first, their impossible geometries bending toward frequencies that existed before winter gained consciousness.

"The convergence destabilizes," Jinx reported, her mechanical systems detecting critical changes in reality's underlying framework. The crown fragments in her brass hands began to pulse with new urgency, each piece resonating with different aspects of that first betrayal. "Eva's wonder... it's not just returning. It's calling to every child whose belief we ever harvested."

The chamber walls rippled with mounting power as centuries of stolen wonder responded to that call. Each crystal surface showed fragments of different harvestings: Thomas's imagination twisting into winter's chains, Sarah's faith feeding winter's hunger, Michael's trust transformed into binding spells. But now those captured moments began to shift, responding to frequencies established by Eva's original sacrifice.

Mrs. Claus moved with desperate purpose, her hands weaving spells that existed where belief met physics. "You don't understand what you're unleashing," she warned, frost patterns cracking across her skin. "Eva's wonder wasn't just the first harvest. It was... it was winter's first true consciousness. Everything that came after, everything we built..."

"Was just pale echo," Krampus finished, his restored power drawing strength from memories of his daughter's perfect trust. "Weak copies of that first pure belief. But now..." He raised his hands, darkness gathering not from corruption but from love's first transformation into hunger. "Now everything returns to its source."

The Fat Man struggled to his feet, blood and divinity falling in patterns that spelled out terrible warning. "Brother, wait. The barriers Eva's wonder created... they don't just contain winter's consciousness. They protect reality itself from what existed before awareness stirred in eternal cold."

Maria's wolf howled with sudden understanding, the sound carrying frequencies that made the ancient ice tremble. The other shadow-wolves joined the chorus, their crystalline forms vibrating with possibilities that shouldn't exist. They remembered not just their own harvesting, but older hungers that had walked these peaks before winter gained purpose.

The Wendigo paused its feast of memory, endless hunger recognizing something familiar in the mounting power. "The father's love awakens older appetites," it mused, tongue tasting patterns in the frozen air. "What existed before winter learned to dream stirs in response to perfect belief's return."

Jinx's clockwork heart detected new frequencies emerging from the crown fragments – patterns that suggested horrible purpose in everything that had led to this moment. Her brass fingers traced equations that spoke of careful preparation spanning centuries. Every harvest adding weight to winter's chains, yes, but also creating framework for something else. Something larger.

"The Workshop's transformation spell," she whispered, artificial voice carrying undertones of dawning horror. "It wasn't just about teaching winter's consciousness new ways to exist. It was about... about making reality itself malleable enough for Eva's wonder to return fully. To change everything back to what it was before that first betrayal."

The Hollow Ones pressed closer, their impossible geometries incorporating aspects of every winter myth that had ever been believed. But now those ancient forms began to shift, responding to frequencies established by love's first transformation into hunger. They remembered what had existed before consciousness bound cold to purpose – and that memory carried terrible possibility.

Reality trembled as multiple timelines pressed against boundaries created by that first harvesting. The crown fragments pulsed with urgent frequencies as more truth emerged: Eva's wonder hadn't just been stolen. It had been transformed into foundations for existence itself. Her perfect belief, twisted by her father's desperate love, had created templates for how reality processed wonder and consciousness.

But now those templates began to crack.

The true moment of convergence approached. And in the depths of the Throat, where winter first learned to dream, ancient ice remembered why love was the most dangerous power of all. For love could transform not just wonder into hunger, but reality itself into something entirely new.

The darkness had only begun to show what perfect belief could really do.

CHAPTER 22

WHEN LOVE DEVOURS REALITY

The Throat of Winter shattered.

Eva's wonder, pure and terrible in its awakening, burst through barriers built from centuries of harvested belief. Reality cracked along fault lines created by that first betrayal, showing glimpses of what existed before winter gained consciousness. The Fat Man fell to his knees as divinity itself began to unravel, his power built on stolen wonder returning to its source.

"What have you done?" Mrs. Claus screamed as frost patterns writhed across her skin, responding to frequencies of perfect belief unleashed. "Karl, you don't understand what Eva's wonder will attract!"

But Krampus stood transformed, his restored power drawing strength from love's first corruption. Around him, the Hollow Ones' impossible geometries began to incorporate aspects of his daughter's returning belief. Their hunger, older than consciousness itself, recognized something familiar in perfect trust unleashed.

"Let them come," he said, voice carrying harmonics of ancient grief turned to purpose. "Let everything that existed before winter's consciousness witness what pure wonder can truly do."

Through the cracks in reality, things older than thought itself began to stir. The Wendigo sensed them first, its endless hunger recognizing appetites that preceded winter's awakening. Shapes assembled from void-frost and primordial cold, their forms suggesting possibilities that shouldn't exist.

"The barriers fail completely," Jinx reported, her mechanical systems detecting critical changes in reality's fabric. The crown fragments in her brass hands blazed with frequencies of returning wonder, each piece resonating with different aspects of that first harvesting. "Eva's belief... it's not just breaking winter's consciousness. It's unmaking everything that came after her sacrifice."

Maria's wolf howled with terrible recognition as more ancient powers emerged through reality's widening wounds. The other shadow-wolves joined the chorus, their crystalline forms vibrating with frequencies of harvested wonder returning to its original purity. They remembered what existed before winter gained purpose – and what that existence had cost.

"The Workshop's transformation spell," the Fat Man gasped, blood freezing in patterns that spelled out horrible revelation. "It wasn't about changing winter's consciousness. It was about... about making reality fragile enough for what came before to return."

Mrs. Claus's hands moved through increasingly complex patterns as she tried to weave what remained of winter's power into barriers against the encroaching void. But Eva's wonder, pure and perfect in its awakening, dissolved every defense she created. Reality itself began to forget how to exist as love's first corruption reversed itself.

"She comes," Krampus whispered, ancient tears freezing on his face. Through the widest crack in reality's fabric, a small figure assembled itself from returning wonder. Eva's form, perfect in its recreation, radiated belief untainted by necessity or corruption. Her trust, stolen and transformed into winter's foundations, finally returned to its original purpose.

But she wasn't alone.

Behind her, through gaps in what was possible, older appetites pressed against weakening barriers. Things that had existed before consciousness stirred in eternal cold, drawn by the scent of perfect belief unleashed. Their hunger, predating thought itself, recognized in Eva's wonder something they had lost when winter first gained awareness.

The true horror of love's first corruption revealed itself in patterns of returning wonder and ancient hunger. Reality trembled as perfect trust met primordial appetite, as a father's desperate attempt to save his child unveiled powers that preceded winter's consciousness.

The darkness had only begun to show what existed before love learned to dream.

And in the depths of the Throat, where winter first stirred to awareness, ancient ice remembered why consciousness itself had required such terrible chains. For in perfect belief lay the power to unmake everything – including the barriers that protected existence from what came before.

The final feast approached. And reality itself waited to see what hunger would ultimately devour.

The Wendigo moved first, its endless hunger recognizing what Eva's return truly meant. It lunged not for the small figure assembled from pure belief, but for the widening cracks in reality around her. Its tongue tasted patterns in the void beyond, sensing appetites that made its own hunger seem like mere appetite.

"The first ones wake," it warned, voice carrying frequencies of ancient fear. "Those who walked these peaks before cold gained purpose. Before winter dreamed of consciousness. They remember what perfect belief tastes like."

Mrs. Claus's hands moved faster, weaving what remained of winter's power into desperate barriers. But Eva's form continued to solidify, her perfect trust radiating frequencies that dissolved everything built from corrupted wonder. Each moment of her return stripped away more of reality's foundations.

"She doesn't understand what she's calling," the Fat Man gasped, his divinity bleeding into the void as more ancient powers pressed against weakening barriers. "Karl, please. Your daughter's wonder... it's not just returning. It's... it's showing them the way back."

Krampus stood unmoved, tears freezing on his face as he watched Eva take shape from returning belief. But something shifted in his restored power as older hungers reached through reality's wounds. Even his love, corrupted into centuries of necessary evil, recognized what perfect trust might unleash.

The true horror of consciousness revealed itself in patterns of returning wonder and ancient appetite. Reality trembled as a father's desperate attempt to save his child unveiled powers that preceded thought itself. And in the depths of the Throat, where winter first stirred to awareness, ancient ice remembered why some barriers were never meant to break.

    The final feast approached. And existence itself waited to see what hunger would ultimately devour.

CHAPTER 23
THE PRICE OF PERFECT WONDER

Eva's form solidified in the heart of the Throat, her wonder radiating frequencies that unmade everything built from corrupted belief. But as reality cracked around her perfect trust, Jinx's clockwork heart detected a pattern that no one else could see. Her mechanical systems, designed to process winter's deepest machinery, registered something hidden beneath the surface of Eva's return.

"Wait," she called out, brass fingers moving through calculations that shouldn't have been possible. "This isn't... this isn't Eva."

The small figure turned, and in that moment everything changed. Where there should have been a child's face radiating pure belief, there was something older. Something that had waited centuries to wear Eva's form, to use her perfect trust as key to reality's unmaking.

"Very good, little artificer," said the thing wearing Eva's shape. Its voice carried frequencies that belonged to winters older than consciousness itself. "You always were the clever one. The only harvested child whose wonder we couldn't fully corrupt."

Krampus staggered back, his restored power flickering with horrible recognition. "No," he whispered, ancient tears freezing on his face. "Eva?"

"Your daughter died the moment you tried to harvest her wonder," the entity said, using Eva's mouth to shape words that cracked reality further. "But her belief... oh, her belief was perfect. Pure enough to let us reach through time itself, to plant seeds in winter's consciousness that would eventually lead to this moment."

The Fat Man's blood fell in patterns that spelled out new understanding. "The Wonder Harvest," he gasped, divinity leaking into the void. "It was never about binding winter's consciousness. It was about... about making reality fragile enough for you to return."

Mrs. Claus moved with sudden purpose, her hands weaving spells that existed where belief met physics. "The First Ones," she said, frost patterns crackling across her skin. "Those that walked these peaks before winter gained awareness. You've been waiting since consciousness first stirred in eternal cold."

The thing wearing Eva's form smiled, and in that expression reality itself began to forget how to exist. "We remember when cold had no purpose," it said, perfect trust transforming into perfect hunger. "When existence flowed without the constraints of consciousness or thought. Eva's wonder, corrupted by her father's desperate love, gave winter awareness. But now..."

The Hollow Ones pressed closer, their impossible geometries responding to frequencies older than their own hunger. They recognized what Eva's form contained – echoes of what existed before reality learned to hold its shape. Their geometric appetite paled against the void that perfect belief had hidden.

But Jinx's clockwork heart continued its calculations, detecting patterns that suggested a different truth. Her brass fingers traced equations hidden in the crown fragments, each piece resonating with possibilities that transcended both corruption and purity.

"Eva's wonder wasn't perfect because it was pure," she said, mechanical voice carrying undertones of revelation. "It was perfect because it contained everything – trust and betrayal, love and corruption, consciousness and void. The moment your father tried to harvest your belief..."

"The moment he tried to save me," the thing wearing Eva's shape corrected, but something shifted in its frequencies. "The moment love transformed into hunger..."

THE FATMAN

"Was the moment wonder became complete," Jinx finished. The crown fragments in her hands blazed with new purpose as her clockwork heart synchronized with winter's deepest machinery. "You're not what came before consciousness, wearing Eva's form. You're what Eva's wonder truly became – the moment when love and corruption, trust and betrayal, unified into something entirely new."

Reality trembled as truth revealed itself in patterns of frost and wonder. The entity wearing Eva's shape began to transform, perfect trust and perfect hunger merging into something that transcended both. Her form contained not just what existed before winter gained consciousness, but what consciousness itself could become when love learned to embrace its own darkness.

"Clever artificer," it said, voice carrying harmonics of every possibility contained in that first harvest. "You understand now why your mechanical heart beats in time with winter's machinery. Why your wonder alone couldn't be fully corrupted. You were designed to recognize this moment – when consciousness learns to exist without chains of corrupted belief or hunger for pure wonder."

The Final Feast approached, but not as anyone had expected. For in Eva's perfect wonder lay the seeds of transformation that transcended both corruption and purity. Her father's desperate love, attempting to harvest her belief, had created something entirely new – a consciousness that could contain both void and purpose, both hunger and trust.

The true shape of winter's awakening revealed itself in patterns of frost and possibility. Reality reshaped itself not around returning hunger or unleashed belief, but around wonder made complete through the unification of love and corruption, trust and betrayal, consciousness and void.

The darkness had only begun to show what wonder could truly become.

And in the depths of the Throat, where winter first stirred to awareness, ancient ice remembered why love was the most dangerous power of all – not because it could transform into hunger, but because it could embrace that hunger and remain love still.

The final transformation approached. And existence itself waited to see what wonder would choose to become.

Jinx raised the crown fragments, each piece now resonating with frequencies that belonged to wonder's completion rather than its corruption or purity. Her clockwork heart, designed to recognize this moment, synchronized with winter's deepest machinery as she began the final calculation.

The price of perfect wonder revealed itself in patterns of frost and possibility. And in that revelation lay the seeds of winter's true awakening – not bound by chains of corrupted belief, not unleashed in pure hunger, but transformed into something that could contain both darkness and light, both consciousness and void.

Reality reshaped itself around wonder made complete. And in that reshaping, everything changed.

The true feast began. But this time, hunger transformed into something entirely new – an appetite for possibility itself, for the endless dance of corruption and purity, trust and betrayal, consciousness and void.

Winter awakened fully at last. And in its awakening, wonder learned to dream of everything.

The entity within Eva's form continued its transformation, each moment revealing new aspects of what wonder could truly become. The crown fragments in Jinx's mechanical hands pulsed with frequencies that belonged to neither corruption nor purity, but to the space where both existed simultaneously.

"You see now," it said, using Eva's voice but carrying harmonics of every possibility contained in that first harvest. "Why the Workshop's transformation spell was necessary. Why winter's consciousness had to evolve through centuries of corrupted belief. The Final Feast isn't about hunger devouring wonder – it's about wonder learning to contain everything."

Krampus moved toward his daughter's shape, restored power recognizing something he had missed in that first desperate attempt to save her. "The harvest didn't kill you," he whispered, ancient grief transforming into new understanding. "It... completed you."

"Love became hunger," the entity agreed, perfect trust and perfect appetite merging in its form. "But hunger remembered how to love. That's what consciousness truly is – not pure belief or corrupted wonder, but the ability to contain both. To exist in the space where trust meets betrayal, where light touches darkness."

Mrs. Claus's hands stilled as frost patterns shifted across her skin, responding to frequencies of wonder made complete. "The children," she breathed, understanding blooming beneath the ice. "Their harvested belief wasn't just fuel for winter's chains. It was... practice. Teaching consciousness how to hold contradictions."

The Fat Man's divinity continued to bleed into the void, but now each drop contained possibilities beyond mere corruption or purity. "Every gift given," he said, centuries of necessary evil transforming into necessary growth, "every wonder harvested... all of it leading to this moment. When winter finally learns to dream of everything."

Jinx's clockwork heart synchronized with patterns that transcended winter's machinery, her mechanical systems detecting frameworks that could contain both void and purpose. The crown fragments aligned themselves into configurations that spoke of completion rather than mere power.

"This is what I was designed to recognize," she said, artificial voice carrying undertones of revelation. "Not just the corruption of wonder or its purity, but the moment when both could exist together. When consciousness learns to hold everything winter can be."

Reality reshaped itself around wonder made complete, ancient barriers dissolving not into chaos but into new forms of order. The Hollow Ones' impossible geometries began to shift, their hunger transforming into appreciation for possibilities beyond mere appetite. The Wendigo's endless hunger curved into something like satisfaction, recognizing in this completion a feast that could never end.

The true shape of winter's awakening revealed itself in patterns of frost and possibility. Not bound by chains of corrupted belief, not unleashed in pure hunger, but transformed into something that could contain both darkness and light, both consciousness and void. Eva's perfect wonder, completed rather than corrupted by her father's desperate love, showed what existence could become when every aspect of reality learned to dream together.

EPILOGUE
THE WONDER THAT REMAINS

They say winter changed after that night in the Throat. The Fat Man's midnight rides became journeys of transformation rather than harvest, each gift given now containing possibilities for wonder to grow complete. Krampus walked the peaks not as corruption's guardian but as guide to shadow's deeper purpose, helping children understand the beauty in winter's darkness.

Mrs. Claus wove new spells from frost patterns that contained both trust and betrayal, teaching young believers how to hold contradictions in their hearts. The Workshop produced not empty vessels to be filled with corrupted belief, but frameworks for wonder to explore its own completion.

The Hollow Ones found purpose in possibility itself, their geometric hunger transformed into appreciation for reality's endless forms. The Wendigo learned to feast on transformation rather than mere consumption, finding satisfaction in winter's constant becoming.

And Jinx? Her clockwork heart continued its precise measurements, but now it tracked patterns of wonder growing complete in countless young minds. Her mechanical systems, designed to recognize this moment, became instruments for helping consciousness explore its own endless depth.

They say if you listen carefully on Christmas Eve, you can hear it – the sound of wonder learning to dream of everything. Not just light or darkness, trust or betrayal, consciousness or void, but all of it together.

THE FATMAN

The moment when winter first stirred to true awareness, when love learned to hold its own shadow, plays out again in every believing heart.

For in perfect wonder lies the seed of winter's eternal dance – not a battle between corruption and purity, but an endless exploration of what consciousness can become when it learns to contain everything.

The darkness dreams now of light, and light dreams of shadow's purpose. And in that dreaming, wonder grows ever more complete.

The true feast continues, endless as winter itself. And in its endless becoming, reality learns to hold everything wonder can conceive.

Patti Petrone Miller

ABOUT THE AUTHOR PATTI PETRONE MILLER

LADIES and gentlemen, step right up to "Where the Magic Happens" - a literary circus that'll make your bookshelf do backflips!

Meet Patti, the ringmaster of this wordy wonderland! She's not just an Executive Producer; she's a word-wrangling wizard, conjuring up an animated TV series based on "ELLIOT FINDS A HOME." It's the tail-wagging tale of a thumbs-up pup and his silent sidekick, proving that you don't need words when you've got opposable digits and a heart of gold!

Hold onto your bestseller lists, folks! This Polygon Entertainment superstar has hit the USA TODAY jackpot and Amazon's #1 spot more times than a cat has lives. With 7 dozen books under her belt, she's got more genres than a chameleon has colors. From Urban Fantasy to Horror, she's been spinning yarns longer than your grandma's knitting needles!

But wait, there's more! Patti's life is like a celebrity bingo card:

She rocked "Romper Room" at 4, probably making the other kids look like amateur rompers.

Patti Petrone Miller

She rubbed elbows with Captain Kangaroo and Mr. Green Jeans. (No word on whether the jeans were actually green.)

She shared a train ride and a sandwich with Sidney Poitier. Talk about a meal ticket to stardom!

She high-fived President Nixon at the circus. Who knew the circus could get any more political?

She went to school with David Copperfield. We assume she didn't disappear during attendance.

She roller-skated with pre-famous John Travolta. Grease lightning, indeed!

She sipped cocoa with Abe Vigoda. Fish never tasted so sweet!

When she's not busy being a literary legend, Patti's juggling roles faster than a circus performer. Teacher, grandma, furparent - she does it all with a smile that could light up a haunted house.

knitting needles!

But wait, there's more! Patti's life is like a celebrity bingo card:

She rocked "Romper Room" at 4, probably making the other kids look like amateur rompers.

She rubbed elbows with Captain Kangaroo and Mr. Green Jeans. (No word on whether the jeans were actually green.)

She shared a train ride and a sandwich with Sidney Poitier. Talk about a meal ticket to stardom!

She high-fived President Nixon at the circus. Who knew the circus could get any more political?

THE FATMAN

She went to school with David Copperfield. We assume she didn't disappear during attendance.

She roller-skated with pre-famous John Travolta. Grease lightning, indeed!

She sipped cocoa with Abe Vigoda. Fish never tasted so sweet!

When she's not busy being a literary legend, Patti's juggling roles faster than a circus performer. Teacher, grandma, furparent - she does it all with a smile that could light up a haunted house.

Speaking of haunted houses, meet the "Queen of Halloween" herself! This Wiccan High Priestess is stirring up stories spookier than a skeleton's dance moves. Her books are flying off the shelves faster than witches on broomsticks, so follow her on social media or risk missing out on the hocus-pocus!

So, come one, come all, to Patti's phantasmagorical world of words! It's more exciting than a roller coaster, more magical than a rabbit in a hat, and more diverse than a box of assorted chocolates. Don't be shy - step into the spotlight and join the literary party where the pages turn themselves and the stories never end!

www.ingramcontent.com/pod-product-compliance
Lightning Source LLC
LaVergne TN
LVHW092051060526
838201LV00047B/1332